Stuck in
NEUTRAL

Stuck in NEUTRAL

Terry Trueman

HarperCollinsPublishers

Library of Congress Cataloging-in-Publication Data
Trueman, Terry.
   Stuck in neutral / by Terry Trueman.
      p.   cm.
   Summary: Fourteen-year-old Shawn McDaniel thinks
his father may be planning to kill him.
   ISBN 0-06-028519-2.
   ISBN 0-06-028518-4 (lib. bdg.)
   [1. Cerebral palsy—Fiction.   2. Physically handicapped—
Fiction.   3. Euthanasia—Fiction.]   I. Title.
PZ7.T7813St   2000   99-37098
[Fic]—dc21   CIP
                                                    AC

Typography by Carla Weise
1   2   3   4   5   6   7   8   9   10
❖
First Edition

For my parents and my sons

ACKNOWLEDGMENTS

First and foremost I want to thank my family. I could not have written this story without the love of Patti and Jesse. Eric Nasburg, Peggy Yurik, Chad and Tami Gardner, Christie Nasburg, Wally and Kathy Egger, and my sister, Cindy Trueman, all read *Stuck in Neutral* at various stages of its development and offered helpful suggestions and support.

Stacie Wachholz helped with *every* aspect of this project; editorially, from the earliest drafts on, her literary judgment was invariably correct. Stacie continues to work with me and help me (a special thanks to her children, Eric and Kati, for letting me steal so much of their mom's time).

There are many friends to thank for contributing to the making of this story, including Leslie Yach and her family and Ginger Ninde. Among writer friends, Michael Gurian and Kevin Gilmore gave thorough, very helpful readings early in the project. Chris Crutcher, Becky Davis, and especially Terry Davis (The Godfather of Y.A. literature in the Inland Northwest) helped tremendously, too. Mark Stimpfle's suggestions and proofreading were worth much more than the steak dinner he got at the Wolf Lodge Inn. Many thanks to my writing teachers over the years: Kay Keyes, Nelson Bentley, Robert Sund, John Keeble, Jim McAuley, and Ursula Hegi.

Antonia Markiet, my editor at HarperCollins, spent hundreds of hours helping me write this story; Ms. Markiet's editorial brilliance and generosity made our collaboration both fun and gratifying. George Nicholson, my agent, in addition to taking care of me in this business better than anybody else could have, has become a good friend. Thanks also to Traci Jersen, Michelle Gladden, and Jade Chan.

So many of my students and colleagues at Spokane Falls Community College were generous with their time and feedback. Among my many students who read this manuscript, I'd like to mention Sherri Fulton, Kei Iwamoto, Brandi Parker, James Barlos, and Sister Mary Eucharista for their contributions. Apologies to all the dozens of other students not named here but who also helped—you know who you are!

For those of you who have been inadvertently left off this list, please forgive me. You know how much you helped. Thank you for making this story possible.

CHAPTER ONE

My name is Shawn McDaniel. My life is like one of those "good news–bad news" jokes. Like, "I've got some good news and some bad news— which do you wanna hear first?"

In the jokes, it's always the good news first, so here goes: I've spent my entire time on planet Earth, all fourteen (almost fifteen!) years I've been alive, in Seattle. Seattle is actually a hundred times cooler than you could believe unless you lived here too. Some people gripe and moan about the rain and the weather, but I love Seattle. I even like the rain.

Our house is about a mile from the Seattle Center, home of the Space Needle, Key Arena where the Sonics play, and the Pacific Science Center. *And* we're only about a mile and a half from Bell

Town, the unofficial former Grunge Capital of the universe. I'm the youngest kid in our family, three years younger than my sister, Cindy, and two years younger than my brother, Paul, who, although I'd hate for them to know I admitted it, are pretty cool for a brother and sister.

Okay, that's good news, huh? Here's some more: I have this weird—I don't know what you'd call it— ability? Gift? Power? Whatever name you want to give it, the thing is that I can remember everything I ever hear, perfectly, with total recall. I mean *Everything! Perfectly! Totally!* I don't know of anybody else, anywhere, who can do this. Most people remember bits and pieces of things they've heard in life, but I've got it all, every sound, ever.

This started when I was three or four years old. At first I could only remember most of what I heard. But by the time I was five years old, everything I heard just stayed in my head. I can remember people talking, TV commercials, every melody I've ever listened to from boring, brain-dead country Muzak to nasty rap lyrics, to the theme music from *Jeopardy!*, to—well—everything: lines from movies, overheard conversations that strangers were having in the street, like—"Well, do you still love him or not?" I heard one lady say this to another lady while they were waiting for the bus in front of our house, and *swoosh* came the sound of the bus along the wet road, and its brakes went *squeal . . . eeeekkk* and the other lady answered, "I don't know. I haven't eaten turkey since he left on Thanksgiving."

For all you know, I might remember, perfectly, what you said to your girlfriend two years ago when I overheard you two fighting outside the Orange Julius at Northgate, or what your dad said to you in Champs when you were ten, and you and he were shopping for a baseball mitt. Remember, you wanted that Ken Griffey Jr. autographed model but your dad said it cost too much. He wanted you to buy a cheaper one made in Taiwan. Your dad said, "Come on, I can write Ken Griffey Jr. right in here," and he pointed at a spot in the pocket of the glove, and you said, "Can you really do that?" And your dad said, "Has the pope got a bullet in him?" And you both laughed. I'm not making it up. It happened. And if I heard you again, even once, after all these years, I'd recognize you, I'd remember your voice, the sound of it, perfectly.

I hope I'm not coming off as conceited here. I'm sure I am. I mean, I *do* think that my hearing memory is kind of amazing, but it's not like it's made me rich or famous. I just happen to have this one talent that I know makes me gifted and special— yuck! I hate that word "special" when it's applied to people. As in "he's a very *special* person." Geez! Who isn't! But the other side of people is true too.

Everybody has negatives about themselves, stuff they wish wasn't a part of them. The bad news about us.

I could go on about my good news for hours, but you probably want to hear the punch line, my bad news, right? Well, there isn't that much, really, but what's here is pretty wild. First off, my parents got divorced ten years ago because of me. My being born changed everything for all of us, in every way. My dad didn't divorce my mom, or my sister, Cindy, or my brother, Paul—he divorced *me*. He couldn't handle my condition, so he had to leave. My condition? Well, that brings us to the guts of my bad news.

One bad news deal is that in the eyes of the world, I'm a total retardate. A "retard." Not "retard" like you might use the word to tease a friend who just said or did something stupid. I mean a *real* retard. Real in the same way that total means *total*. As in *total retard*: Everybody who knows me, everybody who sees me, everybody, anybody who even gets near me would tell you I'm dumb as a rock. Let me illustrate through the wonders of science.

Every year the school district sends out a school psychologist (scientist) to test me for IEPs (Individual Educational Plans). And every year since I was six, the psychologist gives me a bunch of tests ("scientifically normed and standardized"), which are mainly intelligence tests filled with shapes and colors, square pegs and round holes, and "Who was George Washington?" and "What's two plus one?" And every year I sit there and miss every question, fling the blocks into the air or drop them all over or smack myself in the eye with one. Then the shrink goes in and gives my mom a number: I.Q. = 1.2, or mental age 3 to 4 (that's months, not years). Then the psychologist packs up his scientific garbage and moves on to the next dummy.

This has gone on for eight years now. Every year, year in and year out. Yep, according to the world I'm dumb as a fence post. I've heard the docs explain why they think I'm so stupid to my parents and my parents explain it to their friends about a trillion times. They think it's because my brain doesn't work. They don't know that is only partially true.

CHAPTER TWO

The deal is, I have cerebral palsy (C.P.). C.P. is not a disease; it's a condition. When I was born I got brain damaged. A tiny blood vessel burst inside my head and, as luck would have it, this blood vessel was in exactly the 100 percent perfectly *wrong* spot. I don't know enough about the brain to be able to say where in my brain this injury happened (frontal lobe? cerebral cortex?), but wherever it was, it wiped out my muscle control. I can't control *any* of my muscles: not my fingers, my hands, my left foot, my stomach, my tongue, my dick, my throat, my butt, my eyelids, none of them. Not a one. So when the psychologist says, "Who was George Washington?" I can't tell him what I know, from the dollar bill to the cherry tree, from the revolution of the colonists against the British to the father of our country, from his wooden teeth to him knowing Thomas Jefferson to—anything. When I'm asked about the old, dead first prez, all I can do is sit there and drool if my drool function is running, or whiz in my pants if the pants-whizzing gear is engaged, or go "ahhhhhh" if my vocalizing program has clicked in.

Nobody has ever said to me, "Blink your eyes twice if you understand me," or tried to teach me Morse code so that if I could control my neck muscles I might bang out something like "Howdy, I remember everything I hear so would you mind playing a little rock and roll?" Nobody has ever held my hand over a Ouija board or drawn letters with their fingers on my chest. Nobody's ever tried any of these Hollywood-movie techniques of making contact. They think I'm too far gone for that. But the fact is none of these things would work anyhow. They wouldn't work for me because I can't control *any* of my muscles; I've never been able to and I know that I never will. My brain just can't do it. Period. "Blink your eyes if you understand." Well, if I could, I would. I'm trying, like I've tried ten million times before, and it doesn't work; I can't control my blinks. "Bounce your head if you want some chocolate cake." I'd love some chocolate cake, but not only can I not bounce my head, I can't even chew the cake if you shove some into my mouth. I have to just let it sit there and kind of melt into chocolate mush and wait for my swallow reflex to kick in. Swallowing, breathing, flinching, and getting hard-ons, all brain-stem functions, happen to me, but I can't make them happen.

I am in a wheelchair. I can't talk. I can't control my eyes in any way that does me any good, like to read a book or something. First off, I can't hold the book or turn the pages, but even if I could use my hands, my eyes go where they want to go; I can't control them. A lot of the time, luckily, my eyes do focus on stuff and manage to soak up what they're looking at. But it's like my eyes have little minds of their own—I can't will them to pay attention. One second I'll be looking at something and the next moment my eye muscles will decide that the smudge on the wall is where I should be looking, and that'll be that.

I do know how to read; my sister, Cindy, taught me when I was seven years old. I'd sit there looking retarded and Cindy would play Special Education Teacher of the Year. She'd point to letters and sound them out, show me simple sentences, reading the words slowly, like her teacher must have once read them to her. When I'd flip around and vocalize and do my retard number, she'd scold me and then re-peat her lessons. Cindy was playing. I was learning. I picked up reading from Cindy playing school with me, and through remembering sounds, and listening to words spoken as I saw them written down, like on TV screens, video credits, and in real life, from signs of every type, like MOTEL, which taught me m-o-t-e-l, to STOP, which taught me s-t-o-p. Reading is easy once you catch on that every letter just stands for a sound. Once you get that, then the letters on magazine covers and billboards and those just floating across the sky pulled by an airplane or flashing from the Goodyear blimp all turn into sounds. Sounds to letters, letters to words, words to sentences—reading. Of course, nobody knows I can read. Like the captain says in *Cool Hand Luke*, "What we have here is a failure to communicate." In my case that's kind of like calling the Grand Canyon a pothole.

You'd be surprised how much stuff you can learn and remember when you haven't got anything else to do with your time. My main teachers in life are the TV; the car radio; listening to Paul and his friends and Cindy and her friends; eavesdropping on one side of every phone conversation anybody in my family ever has; reading bits and pieces of newspapers, magazines, and books left open on nearby tables, chairs, or couches; catching glimpses of reader-boards, billboards, and a thousand other pieces of written, spoken, seen, heard info from the world. Maybe for somebody who doesn't remember every sound they ever hear, all these things wouldn't mean that much. But I *do* remember everything; *nothing* that ever comes into my head ever gets out again. I'm pretty smart. But this sounds like good news again, doesn't it? Okay, let's get back to reality.

Experiencing life the way I have—that is, only through what I see and hear—has made it hard for me to really understand some things. I've seen people run, but I have no idea what your legs feel like when you do that. What does your arm feel like throwing a baseball? Your fingers holding a pencil? What do your lips feel when you kiss somebody?

Also, sometimes just hearing things can create confusion and misunderstanding: When I first heard my mom talk about "turkey dressing," I wondered why the hell she would dress a turkey. When I first saw a billboard picturing the Marlboro Man, I thought that cowboy up there smoking must be Mr. Marlboro, so for the next six months I thought of my dad as the McDaniel Man, our next-door neighbor, Bob Mayer, as the Mayer Man, the guy who brings our mail as the Postal Man, etc. A lot of these things I eventually figured out, but I'm still confused about some stuff. For instance, how does a car wash work? Do they actually have a bathtub big enough to fit a whole car in there? What about a truck? And doesn't putting the car under the water mess up its engine? And here's one it took me a long time to figure out: Until I actually saw the word written out, I always wondered why nobody realized that calling the killing of sick people "youth-in-Asia" might not be just a little bit offensive to young people in places like Japan and China. Maybe it's a good thing that I can't communicate; otherwise I'd probably act like a fool.

I don't like to feel sorry for myself, but I'm aware of the trouble my condition has put on my family, and I can't help but feel sorry for them. They've all handled it in different ways. My mom is very loving and patient, my sister a lot like my mom. My brother gets impatient and angry sometimes. I wish I could communicate with them to tell them what my life is really all about, but I can't. My condition changed all their lives. It's hurt everyone. Thinking about that is one of the few things that can really bum me out, so I try not to think about it much. I do sometimes wonder what life would be like if people, even *one* person, knew that I was smart and that there's an actual person hidden inside my useless body; I *am* in here, I'm just sort of stuck in neutral. If I think about it too much, I can get real nutso!

My mom, Lindy, still talks to me as if I were a newborn baby or an idiot. She can't know that I understand everything she says to her friends when they drop by to visit her or when she's chatting with them on the phone, everything she says to Cindy and Paul, everything she says period. So my contact with her is limited to "Goo-goo-baby boy-go . . . you a big baby boy . . . boogie woogie googie snoogie." You know, sweet baby talk. I wish just once I could say to her, "Geez, Mom, I'm fourteen friggin' years old." But I can't. That's just how it is.

I try not to spend too much time worrying about how "hard" my life is. Of course, it's kind of difficult not to think about it at least part of the time. What else is there for me to do? For the most part, though, I just live and try not to bitch to myself too much about the bad-news stuff of my life. Bitching doesn't change anything.

Is it frustrating, being trapped inside a useless body? Of course it's frustrating! Have I ever felt frustrated? Hell, yes! But what am I supposed to do? Getting crazy doesn't help. In fact, I figured out a long time ago that the crazier I get, the worse it feels.

There is one final bad-news punch line to my life. This bad news is complicated, difficult to explain. In a nutshell, it's that I am pretty sure that my dad is planning to kill me. The good news is that he'd be doing this out of his love for me. The bad news is that whatever the wonderfulness of his motives, I'll be dead.

CHAPTER THREE

Dead. I'm only fourteen years old. What do I think about death? I'm not sure what I *think*, but I sure know what I *feel*, because I have looked into death's eyes one time, and it was horrible.

Last winter—in early January, just after Christmas— Mom drove us to school one morning. My brother, Paul, a three-letter jock in football, hoops, and baseball, had gone in early for his usual weight training, so it was just Mom, Cindy, and me in the van. We have a wheelchair-loader Dodge Caravan, burgundy. I sat strapped in my wheelchair, which in turn gets locked into these big bolts that hold the chair in place. Cindy sat up front, riding shotgun.

The road shone wet; Seattle drizzle made the

windows on the sides of the van all steamy and beaded with raindrops. I happened to be focusing out the front, through the *clip-clap* slapping of the windshield wipers. In front of us was an older car, an ugly junker, beat-up, dirty, a brownish color.

Suddenly, streaking in from the right side of the road, a dog flew into the path of the brown car. I watched as the dog, twisting and turning under the car, seemed to bend up, flip over, and turn inside out.

In another horrible moment, the back left tire of the car seemed to spit out the broken body. The dog rolled and tumbled along the road several times, tried to right himself, running a couple of awkward, horrible steps to the side of the road, but then collapsed.

Cindy screamed and burst into tears as Mom slammed on the brakes and whipped over to the roadside, sliding in the loose gravel and almost running over the dog too.

Before the van even stopped, Cindy was out of her door and running toward the dog.

"Cindy," Mom screamed. "Cindy!"

But before Mom could even open her car door, Cindy already sat at the dog's side, lifting his head gently onto her lap.

Mom got out of the van. My eyes were only partially focused through the steamy side window.

I watched Cindy sit there on the wet, muddy side of the road. As she stroked the dog's face, I could see Cindy's lips moving, speaking into the dog's ear. It looked to me like tears streamed down Cindy's cheeks.

After only a few seconds the dog began to jerk. Blood gushed out of his nostrils and mouth. Cindy held him still and steady, stroking the side of the animal's face through all the blood.

Suddenly, directly in front of my view, a thick stream of rainwater let loose from the top of the van window, and for a second the glass cleared where I happened to be looking out. In that second I saw, perfectly, the brown eyes of the dog. They were streaked with blood. And in that instant the dog stopped squirming. His body caved in, changing from something terrified and hurt and suffering into—nothing. The dog died. His eyes seemed locked onto mine at that moment when life left him; I wasn't watching a dog then, I was looking at death looking back at me.

Cindy knew it too; in that exact second, her hand stopped stroking the bloody black fur, her lips stopped moving. Cindy let death alone, sliding away from the dog's body, carefully easing his limp head down onto the wet gravel.

There was nothing more to do.

Cindy and Mom got back into the van. We

turned around and began to drive back to our house. Cindy sat smeared in blood, mud, her white Pearl Jam T-shirt soaked, stained, and ruined.

Mom said, "I'm so sorry you had to see this, sweetie."

"No," Cindy answered.

"I mean—" Mom began.

Cindy cut her off. "No, it's all right," her voice low, emotionless. "It was just like I thought it would be."

"I beg your pardon?"

"I mean—death, you know, being so near it. It was just like in that novel *Barabbas* when Lazarus tells Barabbas about death. It was just like that."

Mom said, "A lot of people believe in life after—"

Cindy cut her off again. "No. It's like Lazarus says. Death is nothing, just a big, empty nothing."

Cindy began to cry again. So did Mom. We rode along in silence.

Nothingness, I thought, emptiness. My body breathed evenly, my heart beat slowly. I felt the leather straps on my legs and across my stomach and chest. I remember the sound of the rain, of the tires over the wet pavement, and the feel of the damp air in my throat and nose—emptiness, nothingness.

The thing is my life has always been just in my head. If you think about it, I haven't really got a body. Because of my condition, I get confused about things sometimes. Hearing things, or hearing about things, is different from actually experiencing them. I can imagine what it's like to walk, talk, or sigh, but I don't *really* know. I've seen thousands of people "die" on TV, so I thought I understood what death looked like. But watching that dog lose his life, watching death take his life away, made my stomach weak, my skin tingle, and my heart pound harder in my chest. It made me feel sick.

Death. That was the closest I've ever been to it. I could feel what it was like, which was just like Cindy said—nothing, a big fat nothing. It looked to me like when you die, you just, I don't know, your life just disappears. That day death stared at me through bloody eyes, and it terrified me.

Of course I didn't know then what my dad might be planning. I didn't know then what I know now. Thinking about death again, I get that same sick feeling inside.

CHAPTER FOUR

I guess I should explain about my father, about why I think he's planning to kill me. It's not as though he's stated it directly. It's more an intuition—intuition and a thing that happened last week when my dad stopped by the house.

It was a nice day, sunny and warm. Mom had me out on the deck that runs along the back of our place. I remember that the breeze was kind of tickling my nose and ears. Dad, who hardly ever comes by, showed up, walking through the family room and coming outside to where Mom and I were. He and Mom hugged, and for a moment he didn't say anything to me. Then he walked over and kissed the top of my head. I felt his lips lift a few strands of my hair and the rough palm of his big hand beneath my chin. Dad and Mom began to chat and then the phone rang inside.

Mom disappeared through the sliding glass door, and Dad and I were alone. I remember exactly how many times Dad and I have been all alone together, just the two of us, since he left ten years ago: six times. Exactly six times. This one was the sixth.

Dad began small talk to cover the silence. "How're you doing, big boy?" he asked. "Everything going okay for you? Any hot news for me?" He laughed at his joke, not a big or happy or mean laugh, but a quiet, sad one. Then he leaned over in front of me and brought his face down close to mine. With his brown eyes only inches away from my eyes, it felt as though he were trying to stare through me, straight through my eyes and into my brain. "You're not getting any of this, are you, Shawn?" he asked softly. In fourteen years I've heard him say my name aloud in my presence a total of sixteen times.

Suddenly a big, black crow landed on the telephone line that runs down the alley directly behind the house. It cawed so loudly that it startled both Dad and me. The bird's beady eyes stared at us, its fat black body so huge and heavy that the wire, which held its weight, sagged under it. It cawed loudly once again, then twice more.

Dad looked at the crow and put his hand on my

shoulder, squeezing a little too hard.

"You wanna get at this boy?" Dad said, his voice sounding like a stick breaking. Dad didn't yell, but his voice was cold and hateful.

"You guys peck the eyes out of babies, don't you?" Dad asked. I'd never heard him sound so mad. "You would love a shot at this boy's eyes, wouldn't you?"

The crow cawed again, as though answering Dad's questions. To my dad I'm sure that caw sounded like "Yeah, that's right, what're you gonna do about it?"

"Assholes," Dad muttered, although only one crow sat there staring at him. "Black rainbow, my ass," Dad said, his words low but filled with that same hard anger.

Mom had been drinking a glass of iced tea. The glass sat on a small table on the deck. Dad noticed it there, still half full of melting ice cubes and reddish-brown liquid. Suddenly Dad grabbed the glass and in one frantic, violent motion threw it hard at the crow. "Asshole," Dad grunted again as ice cubes and tea soared out, arcing into the air, and the glass, as if shot from a cannon, flew toward the crow.

The throw had such force that Dad nearly lost his balance. The glass hit the wire, exploding, no more than a foot or two from where the crow perched. Glass showered down onto the pavement below, and the crow quickly unfolded itself; with more of a screech than a caw, it disappeared over the neighbors' rooftops.

Dad watched the crow fly away, looked at the broken glass on the pavement, and breathed deeply and slowly, as if trying to quiet and steady himself.

He turned to me and spoke, the rage in his tone gone, replaced by a sad, slow, tired voice. "What if I hadn't been here?" I could hear his fear. "What if your mom ran in to grab that phone, planning to only be gone a minute or two, and that devil had taken your eyes while she was gone?" He paused again, breathing deeply. "You can't protect yourself at all! How can your mother or I or anybody ever keep you safe? My God, Shawn, you'll never be safe. How can we protect you? You're helpless." He turned away and spoke. "Hopeless." Then he added, so softly I could barely hear, "Maybe you'd be better off if I ended your pain?"

We sat there quietly, and I thought about what my dad had said. I had no idea what he meant, but it made me feel strange and a little nervous, so I tried to put it in the back of my mind.

Mom finally came back onto the deck after she was through on the phone.

"That was for Paul," she said to Dad; then, looking at him, she asked, "Are you all right?"

"No," Dad said quietly, "not exactly. No, I'm not all right at all."

Mom and Dad kept talking. Mom never asked about her iced tea; Dad never mentioned the crow.

But as I listened to them visiting, I knew that my dad *does* love me. It's just my condition that freaks him out, that and my seizure thing.

Did I mention that I have *grand mal* seizures, anywhere from half a dozen to about a dozen every day? Ever since I was born I've had them. When my dad said that thing about ending my pain, he must have meant my seizures. When I was little, they were painful and hard to live with. A big seizure just kind of grabs the inside of your skull and squeezes. It feels as if it's twisting and turning your brain all up and down and inside out. Have you ever heard a washing machine suddenly flip into that *bang-bang-bang* sound when it gets out of balance, or a chain saw when the chain breaks and gets caught up in the gears, or an animal, like a cat, screeching in pain? Those are what seizures felt like when I was little. When I first started having them, I felt like a machine breaking or an animal with my guts spilling out. When I was young, my seizures were really terrible.

And it was back then, when I was little and the seizures were so bad, that my dad was still around. He used to see me having seizures, hold me while

I spazzed out, twisted up, jerked all around, and screamed. I remember when I was about four years old, in the month or so before he left our family, I'd see his face after I'd come back from a seizure and he'd be holding me and his eyes would be so sad-looking. He couldn't stand to see me go through pain. He couldn't bear it. He still can't. But I think it's getting worse. It's like he's going to explode just like that glass did. This incident last week with the crow is the first time I've ever seen Dad act like that. It's so out of character for him, for how I see him and for how the world sees him.

In ways Dad is nothing like he appears to be on all those TV talk shows, and in other ways he's exactly like he seems on them, sincere and smart and compassionate. The truth is that my dad is a complete jerk and a great guy: He is ugly and handsome, charming and cruel, funny and angry. My dad is your basic, slightly smarter than most, human being. He comes fully equipped with a lot of the best and worst stuff available on most models.

My dad is Sydney E. McDaniel. You've probably heard of him, and if you haven't, you've been neglecting your basic daily requirement of TV yap-crap. You know, talk shows. Sydney E. McDaniel: Does Pulitzer Prize ring a bell? Yeah, *that* Sydney E. McDaniel—the one who wrote the poem about him and me that won him a Pulitzer.

CHAPTER FIVE

Lindy felt the early tugs,
Her womb becoming tidal and loud,
the fetus, turning, crying out—
a tiny beast, a braying sigh.
He calls to her. He calls to her . . .
I dream hard the dream of knowing him,
this baby boy coming to us. . . .
A single bird, small, leaps inside my chest,
turning to pure spirit, to pure joy as we watch, crying.
Shawn, he becomes Shawn now,
and that bird inside me wings free too,
wings, wings its way inside me.

I love the beginning of Dad's poem. What's not to love? Who wouldn't enjoy being a witness at his own birth? I love the sound of his words. And I love, most of all, how happy and excited my dad was, how grateful and full of hope at the moment when I arrived. Of course, that's just the start of the poem. Everything soon changed.

Basically, the poem tells about how Dad was never able to deal with my condition; with the "pain" he thinks I experience during my seizures. That's probably one of the reasons he thinks it's all right, even necessary, to kill me. Another is that he thinks I'm a veg.

God, I've always loved that "veg" thing. You've all said it; you know you have. So-and-So is "just a vegetable." The first couple times I heard people saying that, I couldn't figure out what they were talking about. Humans turning into vegetables? It sounded like a horror movie. I wondered, Exactly what kind of vegetables were the people becoming? If it was a redheaded guy, did he turn into a carrot? If it was a cranky Republican lady, did she become a turnip? A gay person into a pink grapefruit? And what kind of people became avocados? Zucchini? Summer squash?

In my father's eyes if I'm a vegetable, a human vegetable, I'll never be able to "enjoy life" or "be productive." I'll never be able to win a Pulitzer Prize, go on talk shows, meet the pope, or have lunch at the White House. I'll never be in *People* magazine, with a three-page story about my life. I'll never attend the Academy Awards, or have dinner with Clint Eastwood, or be hired to write and narrate a documentary on the tragic plight of orphaned children in Romania. I'll never be able to do any of the stuff that Sydney E. McDaniel has gotten to do. So what's the point of my being here if I can't be like him?

This makes it sound like the only reasons my dad would kill me are selfish ones. Honestly, I don't believe that. Dad wants to kill me to save me from suffering. He's afraid I'm trapped and in pain. He wants to kill me because he loves me.

He's enjoyed the success he's had, but it hasn't helped him forget that he's my dad and, therefore, responsible for me. "Shawn," the story-poem, has done just the opposite of helping him "get over" me. Think about it: Dad's fame has made him a professional victim of our relationship; his "pain" over me is the foundation of his career.

If you could hear my dad read the poem aloud, like I have, you'd understand.

I attended the premier reading two years ago at the Kendell mansion. The building used to be a kind of power station back in the old days when Seattle had electric trolley cars. The Kendells bought the place from the city years ago, pumped a couple hundred grand into it, and *voilà!* They had a mansion with 60-foot ceilings and 14,800 square feet of space. I overheard Mom telling Cindy and Paul that Mary

Kendell had long been a supporter of the Seattle arts scene, and that as a friend of Dad's publisher, she offered her home for Dad's reading.

I'm sure my mom didn't want to go, but I guess she felt she had to. Dad had already read the poem to her in our kitchen earlier in the week. I had been in my bedroom, two rooms away, and able to hear only parts of it and then the sounds of them crying afterward. Maybe Mom thought she owed it to Dad to be there at that first public reading. She dressed up that night in a classy, pretty black dress and pearls. She looked beautiful. Unfortunately, she dressed me in dark slacks, running shoes (I can't even walk), a white shirt, a blue blazer and a god-awful, ridiculous *red bow tie*. Geez! I looked like Bing-Bong the Idiot Puppet-Boy.

When the reading started, I got parked in the kitchen in my wheelchair, out of eyeshot of an audience of two hundred of Seattle's artsy-fartsiest folks.

When Dad finished reading, an explosion of applause filled the room. All through the poem I'd heard people crying and blowing their noses, but the volume of applause at the end felt amazingly loud. I jerked in my chair (brain-stem reflex) so sharply that the young waiter who'd been serving hors d'oeuvres and wine before the reading flinched in his chair next to mine. He glanced at me, and my eyes focused on his face. He was handsome and kind-looking, with dark skin and black eyes. I could tell he knew that I was the kid in the poem and that he felt sorry for me.

I remember wishing at that time that I could be him, anonymous and quiet, in charge of my own life. But no sooner had the applause begun to quiet down than here came my mom, her eyes and nose all red. She walked to the back of my wheelchair and rolled me into the living room. Everyone applauded again. Then all these strangers began to come up to me and pat my shoulders and head and back. They all smiled at me, Bing-Bong in my drool-encrusted red bow tie.

The whole scene felt terrible. Being celebrated for something you are not, being completely mis-understood by people who think they're being under-standing, is awful. The people who approached me that evening may have meant well, but they were annoying. The only part of it I liked was the one lady with huge breasts, wearing a low-cut red dress. She leaned over me, her boobs almost falling out, her hands touching my face and her voice cooing. I wanted her to stay right there—my eyes even co-operated for a change—but soon she stood up and went on her way. Most of the rest of the strangers surrounded me and talked about me as though I weren't there, and for them I actually wasn't. The me they talked about, the Shawn in the poem, is not the real me, not even the me my family knows. The kid in the poem is just some cute little redheaded retard named Shawn from my dad's imagination. The Shawn in the poem, my father's version of me, is a paper-thin, imaginary Shawn, a two-dimensional version of Dad's worst fears. It's one thing not to be known for who I actually am, but to be known for who I've never been by a roomful of strangers was the worst.

For all my irritation at the "world premier," I liked, and still like, my dad's poem. I think it is an honest report of what happened to us. I hate to admit it, but I actually like my dad's descriptions of me as a little boy; I sound pretty cute in a gimped-out, C.P. way. I also like seeing my mom and dad together again, even though it's just words in the air from a time long ago. I like a lot of other things about the poem, too. If I'm being honest, and even though I don't like people staring at me, I do like everybody saying my name. I guess I have to admit it, I kind of enjoy being famous.

When the Pulitzer came, I got a kick out of seeing my picture from the book's cover on TV all the time. My dad appeared on twenty-three TV talk shows, news reports, and other programs in the eighteen months following the announcement of the award. It's pretty weird being the country's most famous retard when, with my memory, I bet I'm actually one of the smartest kids anywhere.

My dad, after writing "Shawn," became pretty famous. But the fact is that the poem just made him a professional—what? Victim? Whiner? Abandoning deadbeat dad? Dad left our family because he couldn't stand watching my seizures. Shows what he knows! Did I mention that I love my seizures? That they're doorways to a place at least as real and far better than "reality"? Did I mention that I *love* my seizures? So much for the Pulitzer Prize—just because you win it doesn't mean you know everything.

CHAPTER SIX

As days become a week
and the week draws into a fortnight,
Lindy's mother is holding Shawn
when she sees a movement in his eyes. . . .
I take him into my arms,
stare into his face.
In his eyes there is a quivering,
a strange crackling.
I hold him close. . . .
Everything that was ever going to be,
everything that was going to become,
begins a slow unraveling.

If you saw me having a seizure, you'd swear I was in pain. Maybe part of me is. But the truth is that as much as I love my mom and sister, my brother and father, I'd trade their lives in a heartbeat if it meant keeping my seizures. That sounds terrible, but I can't imagine my life without the wonders of having seizures.

I don't know when a seizure will strike, but when it does, it's like a miracle. When it first starts, it's like a little shock. It begins in my head, just behind my eyes, a small crackling feeling. Then, almost instantly, it shifts into a swirl of color that shuts down my vision; red comes first, then a light blue, which turns slightly darker until it's as though I were looking at the world through dark, blue-tinted sunglasses. Only I'm not looking out at the world, at least at the normal world. The images I "see" are from inside my head. It's as though my eyeballs are turned around backward, looking into my brain, and what I see is everything I've dreamed, experienced, or imagined.

The medicine I am given to control the seizures lessens my muscle contractions, allowing the seizure to affect only my brain. This is great. The bad part of the seizures used to be the way I felt when my muscles would spasm. It felt like I was going to crack apart. But now the medicine keeps my muscles relaxed even as the seizure is happening and protects my body from injury. I've heard that seizures have been known to break bones, including backbones— like I don't have enough problems? That's just what

I need, to be paralyzed with a broken back.

As the seizure continues, I begin to smile and laugh. One of my doctors explained to my mom that this reaction is just an "autonomic, uncontrollable systemic reflex," whatever that is. The doctor said the laughter is just a response to waves of electric impulses flowing through my frontal lobe. Actually I know that my smile and laughter during seizures are really irritating to my family, especially my brother, who hates my seizures almost as much as my dad hates them. I guess it's pretty annoying to be around someone who laughs randomly, just laughs and laughs for no reason at all—I'm sure it kind of rubs it in, just how disconnected I am. But to me the laughter always feels great. It's kind of like what I imagine the giggles must feel like, when everything seems hilariously funny. These laughter moments in my seizures feel like real happiness to me. Why not enjoy them? Think about it: Why should we care whether what makes us happy is just an electrical impulse in our brain or something funny that we see some fool do on TV? Does it matter what makes you smile? Wouldn't you rather be happy for no reason than unhappy for good reasons? All I know, though, is that my electric happiness doesn't help my family much—imagine a world where every time you laughed, everybody else looked sad.

After the smile/laughter part of my seizure has

passed, the room begins to swirl around me, not fast or dizzying, but slowly, allowing me to remember it, see it as it was in the moment before the seizure arrived. Of course, it's not the room out there that is spinning, it is the room in my head; I get a 360-degree view of every detail. What happens next is hard to put into words without sounding like a moronic advertisement for the *Granola New Age Spirit World Gazette*.

The simplest way to describe it is to say that as the room swirls and I finish checking off everything around me . . . well . . . my spirit leaves my body. I hate to say this! I mean, what is a spirit anyway? By saying this, I guess I mean that I accept that we have spirits, and that they can come and go from us. I don't even know that I really believe any of that stuff. But I do know what happens when a seizure comes: As the room finishes its swirling, the blue haze lifts and colors become as sharp and clear as crystals. Then, as my laughter winds down to a slow, steady breathing, a part of me rises from my body. I watch; I guess what I mean is that my spirit watches my bent, unconscious body from some-where outside myself. If it didn't happen to me, I wouldn't believe it.

The first few times my spirit left my body, I was ten years old. It was about the same time that the doctors got my seizure medication just right. When it first happened, it scared the hell out of me; I thought maybe I was dead, and that I'd never go back into my body again. Back then I felt afraid to wander too far away from myself. After a while, though, I realized that as soon as my body awakens from a seizure, I'm forced back inside myself. My little trips have time limits.

I can't make a seizure happen or stop one really, although sometimes, if I concentrate hard enough, I seem to be able to hold it off for a little while. For the most part, though, my seizures are not interested in what I'm doing at the moment they hit; they just kick down the door to my brain, charge in, and make themselves at home.

Of course, except for seizures, my life is one of total dependence. Once I started being able to sneak away from my body, seizures became *very* important to me. I love the feeling of movement, the pure joy of being able to fly. I love the feeling of escaping from my screwed-up, worthless body. I love my seizures because they give me the kind of life I imagine normal people enjoy, and then some. They give me freedom.

When my spirit is out of my body, although I have no physical body, I have complete control of my motions. I do all the things I see and imagine other people do: I soar, sail, walk, run, skip, sit, lie down, roll over, wiggle like a snake, swim like a fish, leap tall buildings in a single bound, slither through cracks in sidewalks and walls, zip over the clouds, whirl like a dervish, dance like John Travolta, sing like Kurt Cobain, and look the world in the eye.

When I'm in a seizure, I go to a different reality. It's like I can do anything I ever wanted to do. I remember touching Cindy's hands as she slept and thanking her for teaching me to read; I remember sitting at the edge of the ocean, digging my toes in the sand, watching whales blow spray and then dive down into the black water. I remember yelling in my dad's ear telling him I was okay. I remember kissing my mom's cheek and cuddling her. All these memories are hazy, as if coated in that filmy stuff that photographers use to make homely people look pretty in studio photographs.

Are these memories of real things or imagined ones? I don't know. Are your dreams real or imagined? You don't imagine a dream, do you? I don't know what's real or what's imagined when I have a seizure, and to tell you the truth, I don't care.

All I know is that my seizures are a nice part of my life, a part I love. Seizure trips are as real to me as sitting in this wheelchair right now, remembering, in perfect detail, two months ago when I heard the sounds of the furnace humming and my brother talking on the phone to one of his friends about getting a pizza and a half rack a brewskies. My seizures are as real as my schooling and a lot more sane. Did I mention that I go to school? Oh yeah, absolutely. In fact, it was at school yesterday that I had to face the fact, again, that my dad might be thinking about killing me.

CHAPTER SEVEN

Shawn does not grow,
he stays the same. . . .
His arms and legs
are overcooked spaghetti
laced with the bones of dead birds. . . .
Behind his eyes it's blank
as fog over snow.

School. The retards' class. Jeez, what a friggin' zoo. The Severely/Profoundly Handicapped Special Education Program at Shoreline is an amazing piece of work. There are only seven of us kids in the room, along with our teacher, Mrs. Hare, and two teacher's assistants, Becky and William. William is this incredibly cruel, vicious psychopath with huge hairy arms who tortures us and does terrible things to us whenever we're alone with him . . . did that get your attention? I'm just messing with you.

Actually, William is an incredibly nice guy. He's about fifty and real strong and big. He's great. Once William accidentally broke my arm when I was falling out of my wheelchair. He grabbed me as I was nose-diving toward the hard tile floor; he didn't want me to crack my skull, so he grabbed me, catching my arm at the wrong angle. I was in the middle of a seizure when it happened, but I came back into my body pretty fast when that bone snapped. Of course, there was a big-deal Incident Report and William had to answer a lot of questions, but he never treated me any differently than he always had; he was just as nice as always. He's not afraid of us retards.

Becky is great too. She has red hair, long and soft. She's only about twenty years old and her body's gorgeous and she's super nice. I love it when Becky works with me, especially when she wears a low-cut top and has to bend over to load and unload me from this special standing contraption they put me in a couple hours every day. Her breasts are perfect: round and smooth and big. If I could be William, I'd spend every hour of every workday trying to figure out how to score with Becky. Hell, I'm *me* and I do that already, but you'd have to figure William would at least have a chance. I mean, he speaks the same language as Becky, and can walk around and smile and do all of those necessary prerequisites to scoring. You'd figure the guy would have at least a chance. But I've never seen anything sexy or weird ever going back and forth between them. For some reason that makes me like William even more.

Mrs. Hare is an older teacher lady, little reading glasses hanging on the end of her nose. She always looks like she just got back from a walk on a windy day. She's nice, patient, a little boring but real caring. I don't like her quite as much as I like William and Becky, but she does a good job running the show. And what a show it is.

I'm making this all sound normal and sane. Mrs. Hare and William and Becky are fine, but that's where normalcy and sanity end. The zoo is not like any other schoolroom you've ever seen. Although we're located at Shoreline High School, we're not really a part of it.

First of all, remember that we students are all retards.

We moan, we drool, we take dumps in our pants. We smack ourselves upside our own heads. We take headlong swan dives into the floor. We eat dirt and eraser dust and hunks of old crayons and chalk, anything, actually, that we can get into our mouths. Those of us who can walk, walk into walls and doors and one another; those of us who can't walk just sit around "ahhhhhhhhhhhing" all day long. Teachers call this "vocalization." And when you've got half a dozen retarded teenaged vocalizers all "ahhhhhhhhh-ing" at once, the noise is pretty unbelievable.

In order to qualify to be in our class, you have to demonstrate lack of continence, meaning you can't control your expulsion emulsions; in other words, you're too messed up to know how to use the bathroom on your own. The smells in the room are pretty amazing; Lysol Meets the Pigpens in *Beyond Thunderdome*.

I'm pretty sure I'm the only secret genius in our group. Pretty sure. You never know. It probably sounds like I think I'm better than the other retards. Maybe I sound cruel to talk about us the way I do. Well, I absolutely don't think I'm better. I don't think there's some kind of retard ranking, with me on top and all the little stupids below me. I use the word "retard" the way I use any word or words: dolphin, racehorse, sandwich, sidewalk, and apple. Is a dolphin better than a racehorse? A sandwich better than a sidewalk? An apple better than a whatever? Words just stand for the things they are and for what people mean them to stand for. A retard is not a normal person. Putting us in baseball caps and Reebok high-tops and teaching us to connect bolt A to nut B, to count back change, to stack plastic-covered packages of pork chops, none of these things will make us normal. Making us try to copy normal people's values, habits, hobbies, and traits will not change the fact that we retards are not normal folks. *We are different!* I call my classmates retards because that's the word people use when they look at us. Retard means "slow," but it's also a word used for a whole class of human beings who are only slow because normal people try to make everybody do things in the same ways and at the same pace. We retards are retards only because normal people call us that.

I actually enjoy the weird irony of the fact that I'm considered the dumbest kid in my retard class. Most of the others can talk a little, some walk a little. All but me communicate at least a little bit. One guy, Jimmy, walks around saying "honey" all the time. Several kids are able to ask for cookies. Another guy, Alan, constantly grabs his crotch and says "winky" over and over.

Our classroom looks like a torture chamber or a weirdo's playpen. Of course there's all the useless standard school crap: pictures of presidents, big alphabet letters, maps, a chalkboard, a closet, a Kleenex box. But if you look a little closer, you can't help but notice the number of leather straps on odd, rack-looking wooden contraptions, soft cords (used to hold us kids in place), some beanbag chairs, a large couch mysteriously stained, and a wide variety of bizarre objects used for "educational purposes."

My school. And darned proud of it. Fight on, you mighty Spartans! Fight on! Rah! Rah! Rah!

I was having a pretty good morning yesterday until my dad showed up with a video cameraman from Channel 7, the local PBS station.

Although I'm sure my dad would have preferred to talk with Becky, he walked into the room and over to Mrs. Hare. He introduced himself and they chatted. It looked like Mrs. Hare had been expecting them. She smiled and he smiled and my classmates and I drooled.

The tall cameraman guy with a beard, who had come in with Dad, began setting up his video camera. Dad glanced around the room, then started a little "Testing, one, two, three . . . testing one, two, three" routine into his microphone. He walked over to me and patted my head, then bent over and kissed my cheek.

"Is that where you wanna shoot?" the cameraman asked.

"Sure," Dad answered.

"Is our sound right?" the cameraman asked.

"Yep," my dad answered.

"We're rolling," the cameraman said.

"Okay," Dad said; then he took a deep breath.

"Hello," he said, holding the microphone in

front of him, looking straight into the camera. "I'm Sydney McDaniel, and this is my son Shawn. Shawn is profoundly developmentally disabled. I'm here with him today at his school. You might not be aware of it, but your tax dollars, to the tune of thirty-five thousand dollars a year in services, staffing, special equipment, and a wide variety of additional expenses, are used to support each and every uneducable child, like Shawn, in programs designed to educate the uneducable. That's thirty-five thousand dollars per child, per year, year in and year out. If 'educating the uneducable' sounds just a little too paradoxical to you, well that's exactly why we're here today, at Shoreline High School. We've come to visit my son and honestly examine just what your money is buying."

I sat listening to and remembering Dad's words; in the background I could hear "winky, winky, winky" and "ahhhhhhhhhh," and, "honey . . . honey . . . honey." William came into my sight, and he looked angry.

Dad continued, "While none of us would disagree with the noble intentions of the State Department of Education, and the Seattle Public School District, that each and every child deserves an education designed to help that child achieve his or her greatest level of accomplishment and potential, the fact is that our schools, *your* schools, are paying hundreds of thousands of dollars a year making sure that children who simply *cannot* learn are being 'taught.' Why do we *teach* children who cannot *learn*? Is it really worth the allocation of resources presently deployed to help a fourteen-year-old kid master tying his shoes and spelling 'cat,' when such tasks require hundreds and hundreds of hours of individual teacher time? And, even worse, how exactly do we justify the price we pay in energy and resources for a child like Shawn, who will *never* tie his own shoes or speak or understand the word 'cat,' much less *spell* it?"

You have to agree, Dad made some interesting points. Why educate the uneducable? Why even try? Remember, in the eyes of the world, based on proven scientific methods for judging such things, I'm an idiot. A moron. A celery stalk. A chunk o' granite. My classmates aren't exactly on track for careers in nuclear physics or brain surgery either.

My dad turned slowly toward me, then gazed back into the camera. "If we cannot educate kids because they are uneducable, and we will not simply warehouse them in shoddy group homes or huge, impersonal, neglect-prone institutions, doesn't it ask the question, 'What do we do?' I wish I had a simple answer for such questions. We all wish we had simple answers to our complex questions. Yet the truth is there are no simple answers—there are only complex answers to complex ques . . ."

Right there was when my seizure hit.

It came on right when my dad and me were in front of the camera looking all cozy-lovey father and son like, right then—*crackle-crackle-crackle-swoosh*—red light, blue light, bluer light—idiot laughter—muscle contractions—slow spin of the room—spirit rising out of my body.

And while I don't usually remember many details of "reality" during seizure times, I do remember parts of this one.

Dad stopped talking when he heard me laughing. He turned, looked in my eyes, saw the seizure grabbing me. Of course I felt happy, as I always am when a seizure hits, but I caught glimpses of his face, his mood, as I drifted away. He looked sad and disappointed. Because I was having a seizure, I couldn't make out all of what he said, but bits of his speech came through: "And what of our children who suffer unbearable pain . . ." "doesn't to love them . . ." "if we really love that child . . ." "shouldn't we . . ." "and if . . ." "no hope . . ." "shouldn't . . ." "someone . . ." "end his pain?"

My spirit floated near my dad and me. I listened as well as I could, trying to pay attention. But in another moment my spirit was unable to resist the temptation to cruise over and nuzzle Becky's breasts, to lick the vanilla cookies in the open bag on Mrs. Hare's desk, to soar out to the playground and play slalom between the posts of the swings and the metal poles of the basketball backboards.

I know, I know, I'm irresponsible. I should have tried to stick around and listen to the rest of Dad's PBS special on retards and educableness and "Appropriate Allocation Decisions in an Era of Diminishing Funding." I should have stuck around. So sue me. Hell, I'm fourteen years old! For some reason, flying and slaloming and cookie licking and breast nuzzling just felt like a much better— what?—utilization of my resources.

When I came back into my body, Dad and the cameraman were already packing up their gear. The show was over. I felt a little bad about missing it all. And then I remembered what my dad had said: "end his pain. . . ."

I'd heard that phrase not so long ago, that day with the crow. At that time it had made me nervous, but I'd tried to forget about it. Now, hearing it again so soon, I got the picture.

In another few moments Dad walked away, toward the door. As he reached for the door handle, he glanced back over his shoulder one final time. I happened to be looking directly at him. There was something in his expression that I'd never seen before, a look in his eyes that I can't describe. All I know is that I felt a chill, as though a sudden gust of cold air were blowing through the room.

End my pain? It made me mad. What right does he have to decide what's best for me? What right does he have to think about ending my pain? He's never even around me! Dad is only talking now, but how long before he does more than just talk?

CHAPTER EIGHT

I say,
why is this happening to us?
Lindy shifts Shawn in her lap,
slides her fingers across his cheek,
gently as soft breathing.
She doesn't answer.
We sit in silence
and we wait.

I barely remember when Dad left our family. I wasn't quite four years old, but I remember the last time he ever fed me, and that was the same week he left us.

"Damn," Dad yelled as I coughed a mouthful of rice and mashed vegetables into his face. He was feeding me my lunch.

Mom was doing dishes.

"I can't get used to this," Dad hollered as he wiped my spit and bits of food off his face. "I'd expect it from a baby! But you're a little . . . Damn it!" he yelled again, throwing the spoon across the kitchen into the wall.

"Hey," Mom said.

Dad's hands trembled as he looked at her.

"I'm sorry," he said, his voice tired and sad.

Silence then.

Mom said, "I know, babe, I understand. We just have to try and remember it's not his fault."

"It's not *him* I'm mad at," Dad said. "It's that damn screwed-up part of him, that stuff he can't help but is all we ever see! Maybe it's God I'm hating so much."

Mom stared at Dad from across the room, her face full of sadness.

Dad said, "Why does he have to be so totally messed up? Why does God have to make him such a total wreck?"

"It's not God," Mom said softly. "You don't believe in God anyway, but if you did, you'd know it's not God. It's just the way things happen sometimes."

"I know," Dad said, his voice low and tired, "but I can't do this anymore. I can't stand this."

Mom looked at Dad for another moment, then turned away. "I don't want to hear it," she said, mad, low, and icy. Dad just sat there.

• • •

I also remember one time when I heard my mom talking about Dad's leaving. Mom sat with her friend Connie. They drank coffee at the little dining area just off our kitchen. I sat in my wheelchair in my usual spot next to the window overlooking Puget Sound. It was a pretty day, blue sky and a clear view of the Olympic Mountains far across the water.

Mom sounded very sad. "I understand him," she said, talking about my dad. "I know what he went through over Shawn. The thing that kills him is not knowing whether Shawn is aware or not. The doctors have assured us, a thousand times, that it's almost impossible that Shawn could have any awareness, but it's that 'almost' that makes it intolerable for Syd."

Connie said gently, "I still don't think that gave him a right to leave you guys."

My mom looked down into her coffee cup. "No," she said. "It sure didn't. He's weak and cowardly. Sometimes I hate him. But I know, too, that he just can't stand seeing Shawn suffer with the seizures. Syd can't stand the thought that Shawn might be trapped inside himself."

Even before Dad won a Pulitzer for "Shawn," he'd won awards. His books of poems, writings in newspapers and magazines, and teaching literature at the college where he used to work made him seem smart to me. Does he know something that I don't about dying? Would he kill me without being sure it was the right thing to do? Knowing that my dad loves me makes everything even more confusing.

Not that it's important, but my dad and I both have double-jointed thumbs. We can bend them backward, at an odd angle, so they look as if they've been broken by a mafioso enforcer. Neither Paul nor Cindy can bend their thumbs backward like that, but I can. Actually, when I say I can bend my thumbs, what I mean is that on those few times when Dad comes to visit, he always takes my hands and gently bends my thumbs back, so they look broken and weird. Then he puts his thumbs like that. I can't control the muscles of my own thumbs, of course, but Dad holds them at that strange right angle; then, while he's holding my thumbs like that, he bends his own back too. Our hands, except for the difference in size, look like the paws of mutant monkey twins, half human, half deformed. It's funny. I've watched Dad's face come into focus sometimes in the middle of this little ritual, and it's always seemed that it's then that he feels closest to me. Sometimes he laughs sadly, a real small laugh. And right then I feel most loved by him.

I almost trust Dad to do what's best. I almost trust him to know whether "ending" my "pain" would be the right thing to do. Almost.

CHAPTER NINE

Inside my chest,
where my heart should be,
a ghost bird
is flying into a terrible wind,
a frozen winter wind,
and its eye is covered in ice,
and it has no voice,
and it is fading out of itself;
falling and falling.

Cindy's sleepovers with her girl friends are one of the few places where invisibility has advantages. Being a total retard and not being able to communicate has presented certain drawbacks when it comes to securing a close, intimate relationship with a girl.

In fact, in case you couldn't figure this one out on your own, it's made it completely impossible. Nope, I'm never gonna score with the ladies, that's for sure. But like I said, invisibility has some advantages.

After a little while of being with me, people begin to forget I'm there. First they look past me, then around me, and eventually right through me. I become invisible.

However, every dark cloud, as they say—you wouldn't believe the stuff teenage girls talk about when they think no guys are around to hear. And because I can't tattle, and because they think I'm a vegetable anyway, they don't think of me as a guy. Actually I'm pretty sure they don't think about me much at all.

There they are, bouncing around in their bras and panties and changing clothes right in front of me in the family room. Not really "right in front of me," but from where my wheelchair is parked, near the window in the kitchen, when my eyes happen to turn that direction, I have a perfect view into the family room. Our big-screen TV, the CD player and stereo, and a couple of big couches are in there, so that's the room where Cindy and her friends usually camp out for the night. The way our house is set up, although I'm in a different room altogether, I'm only about fifteen feet away from them. I can hear all but their most private, softly whispered secrets. And when my eyes are willing, I can watch them.

Tonight Cindy has a new friend over for the first time. She's come for a sleepover. Most of Cindy's friends are pretty cute. But none come close to being as pretty as this girl is. She is tall, and she has blondish-brown hair and an amazingly attractive body. Her face looks like one of those women in Maxfield Parrish paintings (Mom has a couple prints in her room). God, she's beautiful.

When people first meet me, they usually do their Annie-Sullivan-meeting-Helen-Keller-in-*The Miracle Worker* routine.

"HI SHAWN, NICE TO MEET YOU. . . . MY NAME IS ALLY WILLIAMSON. . . . HOW ARE YOU?" For some reason people always speak real slowly and real loudly when they're introduced to me. Usually it bugs me. Not with Ally Williamson, though. She's *so* perfect!

Cindy says, "He doesn't talk."

Ally answers, "Oh. Well . . . does he . . . understand . . . does he know what I'm saying?"

Cindy says, "Not really."

Ally turns back to me. "HI ANYWAY, SHAWN. HAVE A NICE DAY."

Looking at Ally, listening to her, my stomach aches and is warm and safe all at once. My palms are sweaty. My chest, my heart, all my insides feel hot and tingling. I won't even start to describe some of the other parts of my body—other than to say that I feel better than I've ever felt. I feel dizzy.

Two hours pass and I'm in bed in my room, thinking about girls in general and Ally Williamson in particular. My bed is an oversize crib with wooden rails to keep me from falling out onto the floor.

I can't hear Cindy or Ally talking anymore and the TV is silent, so I'm pretty sure they are already asleep in the family room. It feels late; the whole house is quiet. A soft breeze blows some branches against my window. Even in the darkness, I can "see" my room. Above my head a cardboard African animal mobile hangs over my bed. This "stimulation" piece was installed before I could remember anything, which means before I turned four. My dad may have put it here. How many times have I looked up at that giraffe, tiger, lion, parrot, zebra, and hippopotamus? How many times? Well to give you some idea: The giraffe has a total of 76 spots on his body from the tip of his ears to the bottom of his hooves; the zebra, 38 stripes; the tiger, 23. The lion shows six teeth and has 122 visible brush strokes making up the long, tan hairs in his mane; the hippo shows only eight teeth in his huge, gaping mouth; the little bird perched on the hippo's ass has four yellow-tipped feathers on its wings. I could go on. The point is I've put in a lot of lying-here-staring-at-the-mobile time in my life. Even through the dark I can "see" all the mobile's features.

Finally, unable to hold off any longer, I feel myself starting to drift toward sleep.

My bedroom, despite being black already, turns darker still. The room begins to swallow me, like it does every night. My immobile mobile hangs in the stillness; my plastic foot brace jobbies that I wear to keep my feet and ankles less spazzed out lie on the floor; soon all of the room and everything in it fades into the darkness.

As sleep takes me, I begin to dream. In my dream I take a deep breath, and I have complete control of my body; it's similar to the feeling I have when I'm in a seizure.

I dream about Ally. I am alone with her and we begin to kiss. It feels great. Even though we don't know each other, somehow we're in love. I wonder where we are; the room doesn't seem familiar. I think about where I'd like to be, and an instant later we are sitting on the top of the Space Needle in downtown Seattle, six hundred feet above the city. Our legs dangle over the side. We face east, looking out past the hills leading up to the mountains. The sun is rising over the tallest peaks of the Cascades. The horizon, the huge length of it, is blazing in pink, red, and orange. The mountains look purple and blue, the snow tinted by the colors. There is such a huge feeling to this sunrise, like all the universe spreads out from the light, and the entire universe looks back toward it.

"God, this is beautiful," Ally says.

We sit holding each other, the morning's first light covering us.

Ally whispers again, "It's so beautiful."

"I love you," I say to Ally. She is the first girl I've ever said these words to. And even though I'm only a kid, even though I'm young and inexperienced and I know it would sound stupid and corny, I almost add, "Darling."

"I love you too," Ally whispers back; then she pulls herself close to me. It feels as though we are blending together, I can't tell where I end and she begins. Then Ally says, "I love you, my darling."

Suddenly, even though I know that I am only dreaming, I feel so loving, I feel so loved, that I begin to cry.

When I wake up, there is a fly on my face. I can feel its tiny feet moving across my cheek. It is looking up my nose. Every few moments its wings lift it off me and I think it's going to go away, but quickly it returns. Of course, there is nothing I can do about it. I can't move my head or my hands to shake it off or swat it. I can't holler for help. This has happened a lot of times before and I really hate it. All I can do is lie here and try to think other thoughts. I focus on last night.

I can't remember exactly how or when my dream

of being with Ally ended. I had started to cry—dream crying, not real tears. She had held me close to her, dream holding, not our real bodies.

The next thing I knew, it was morning, and I was waking up in my bed: real self, real body, real breathing. I was lying here quietly, relaxed and fantasizing, when this damn fly arrived. As it rises from me, I can see its bulbous blue eyes, hear the annoying, torturous *buzzzz* of its wings. Then I feel it land again, crossing my face, over my cheek, onto my lips, pausing at the corners of my mouth. Is it feeding? Laying eggs? Soon it wanders up into my eye; I blink, an involuntary but appreciated reflex.

Dreaming about Ally, about being with her, was wonderful. Before last night, when I'd think about Dad killing me, my fears were based on what I guess everybody fears about death, just not knowing what's coming next. Before last night, I only worried that there might not be life after we die. Of all people I guess I should know, because of my spirit travels, that we are more than just our bodies and our brains. I should believe that we have souls. Yet I'm still not sure. Before, it didn't matter so much if Dad's deciding to kill me might stop everything. Now, for some reason it matters a lot! If feeling the way I felt with Ally is this nice, how many other wonderful things might I still get to feel someday?

I can't stop thinking about love. I've never been

in love before. I know my mom and dad love me. They're required to by all the rules of doing the right thing. They love me, but they don't really know me, and they never will. They can't. If it hadn't been for me, Mom and Dad might have stayed together. I think about Cindy and Paul. It's the same thing for them; I'm sure they love me, but how can they not feel resentment toward me? I ruined our family. Whatever their feelings, they don't know me; they've never known me. For the first time in my life I'm thinking about being loved and being known somehow going together. What if somehow, some way, I could get somebody to love me and know me? What if there is a way that I could let somebody know that I am smart and that I like my life and that I don't want to die!

If my dad walked into this room right now and killed me, no one would ever know what I was really like. I want to love someone, and feel loved in return, for my real self. What if someone loved me enough to somehow break through and discover that I'm inside this body? That I am in here? Maybe that person could tell my dad what my world is really like and that I'm not in any pain. Aside from everything else, if I were loved enough to be truly known, maybe that could save my life?

CHAPTER TEN

Something is happening;
Lindy won't look at me,
and I can't look at myself. . . .
Words,
once real as firewood or concrete . . .
become meringue of dust.

Breakfast time. When I eat, I know that it's not a very pretty sight. It's the same every morning. Mom pulls up the kitchen chair she always sits in when she feeds me and places my bath towel–size "bib" around my neck. Then she scoops oatmeal into an ancient green plastic Teenage Mutant Ninja Turtles bowl (Donatello). She always uses this bowl, I think because she can hold it by the turtle's head up close to my face and spoon the mush into my mouth.

Putting food in my mouth is only the first step to feeding me. I can't voluntarily swallow, so we have to wait for my swallowing reflex to kick in. Because of this, half the food oozes back out before any of it goes down. Mom has fed me practically every meal I've ever eaten, so she's an expert. She shovels a spoonful in, then leaves the spoon under my lower lip, resting it lightly on my chin until half the food slides back out, then she spoons it in again, repeating the procedure as many times as it takes until my body manages to swallow. Then I get the next spoonful. It takes a while to feed me. I cough and spit a lot too, spraying my meals, like that time with my dad. I know I must look terrible. I'm glad Ally left before I got up.

This morning Mom seems distracted. She lets more oatmeal than usual slide out of my mouth and down onto the bib. She keeps running her fingers gently across my chin, wiping away the drooled cereal. There is something in her expression, something in her eyes, that tells me something is wrong.

When I'm done eating, after Mom has gone to the bathroom and washed the sticky oatmeal off her hands, she comes back into the kitchen and calls for Cindy and Paul, who are both upstairs.

"Yo," Paul calls back.

Cindy doesn't answer.

"Cindy!" Mom calls again, louder.

"What?" Cindy answers.

Mom says, "I need you both down here for a second."

Mom stands leaning against the wall between the kitchen and the family room. I happen to be looking at her. She looks pretty. Even though she's forty-five years old, she looks good. Mom's real name is Linda, but my dad gave her the nickname Lindy back before they were even married. It's stuck with her ever since. Watching Mom standing there, I remember so many things about her: I remember every soft word she's ever whispered in my ear, every gentle, silly lullaby, each and every time I've come back after a seizure to find myself cradled in her arms. If I had to name a single reason why I've been as happy as I've been, I know that it would be my certainty of Mom's love for me, love that's absolute, rock solid. Yet right now, at this moment, I think about Ally and how much I'd like to have a girlfriend. I even wonder what it would be like to love someone else more than I love my mom. I know that the secret to happiness is love, to be loved the way Mom has always loved me, and to love back the way I've loved her. Yet now, somehow, I think about a new meaning for love, something even bigger.

Cindy and Paul show up together, coming into

the family room, pushing and teasing.

"I need to tell you guys something," Mom says. She uses her best put-on-a-happy-face voice, so all of us know instantly that something must be wrong.

"I need to discuss something with you guys," Mom says.

"You said that," Paul counters, already on the defensive.

Both Cindy and Paul look guilty, not specific guilt, but more like "I wonder what she's found out about?" Mom notices this and laughs. "You're not in trouble," she reassures them. "I just have to tell you something."

By this time I can feel the weight of what's coming. I can hear it in her tone. Mom's a naturally positive and cheerful person. When she sounds as overly positive as she's sounding now, it has to mean something is pretty bad.

"What's going on?" Cindy asks anxiously, staring at Mom with the same suspicious feelings I have.

"It's about your dad," Mom says.

Paul instantly groans and asks, "Now what?"

"I haven't even told you what it's about," Mom says defensively.

Paul snaps back, "If it has to do with Dad, you don't have to." He slumps down on the big blue couch in the family room. Cindy sits next to him.

Mom takes a breath, and she turns to Paul.

"You're mad at your dad. I know that, but you need to set that aside for a moment and just listen. *The Alice Ponds Show* is going to do a program about your dad's newest project—"

Cindy interrupts. "The thing about the schools?"

"No," Mom says.

"What new project?" Paul asks.

Mom sighs, just a quick little sigh, but all three of us catch it. It's her signature giveaway that the punch line is next.

"Your dad's writing a new book. It's about Earl Detraux."

"Oh no!" Cindy snaps, jerking her knees up to her chest and burying her head.

"Who?" Paul asks sarcastically. "Who's Earl Dayglow?"

Cindy's voice comes out from her knees. "Has Dad gone crazy?"

Mom says, "Your dad thinks it's an important story. He thinks—"

Cindy interrupts. "Bull! He's not thinking at all. Jesus Christ!"

Paul yells, "What's going on?! Who's this Earl guy?"

Cindy looks up and hisses, "He's that monster from eastern Washington who murdered his kid."

I placed the name immediately, the second Mom said it, and now the voice-overs of a dozen TV news stories flash back perfectly in my head: Earl Detraux killed his brain-damaged two-year-old son, Colin, a little over a year ago. He smothered the little boy and was convicted of second-degree murder. He received a twenty-year sentence in Walla Walla State Penitentiary.

Mom answers Paul, telling him about Earl.

"I don't get it," Paul says. "Why's Dad into that?"

Mom says, "I won't speak for your father. I'm not going to stand here and lie to you and say that I understand or agree with everything he does. I think your dad believes that families like ours, families with kids like Shawn, are not very well understood. Your dad's work, his writing and his projects, are about trying to get people to think about what happens when a child like Shawn comes along." Mom pauses a second. Her face is sad and suddenly she looks real tired. I think about all the times that I've heard her on the phone talking with Dad, crying, criticizing, and arguing with him. "Your father just wants you to know that he'd appreciate your cooperation for this project."

Cindy snaps, "Cooperation?!" She sounds mad.

Mom adds, "He wants you both to know that if you want to, you can join him on the program and talk about life with your brother. The people at *The Alice Ponds Show*—"

Paul's burst of angry laughter interrupts Mom. "Right! Alice Ponds. I'd rather have ground glass pounded up my nose!"

"Paul," Mom says, pushing down a nervous laugh.

"Join him?" Cindy asks angrily. "Why?"

Mom pauses a moment before she speaks. "I think your father believes that his work might help other families with kids like Shawn. I believe that your dad feels that kids like Shawn and their families need a lot more from society than volunteer stints with the Special Olympics. He knows that the problems that families like ours face are a lot more complex than they are presented on feel-good made-for-TV movies. Your father—"

Paul interrupts again. "My father is a hopeless jerk, and I wouldn't help him do *anything*, least of all go on a freak show and talk about my brother." Paul pauses a moment; then he adds angrily, "Alice Ponds? Alice Friggin' Ponds!"

Paul's been mad at Dad for years, ever since he left us. Not all the time—they've tried to iron things out—but the peace has never lasted longer than a few months. Paul always finds something to get upset about and then refuses any contact with Dad. These days they're not speaking at all.

Mom says, "It's completely up to you guys, whether you want to go on *Alice Ponds*. Your dad would never make you, and, of course, neither will I.

When your dad talked to me about this, he mentioned that the *Alice Ponds* producer wanted you guys on the show, but your dad didn't even ask me to ask you. He just wanted me to let you know that the invitation was there. If you want to go, you can; if you'd rather not, you shouldn't."

Cindy asks quietly, "You think Dad really cares about other people with kids like Shawn?"

Mom answers right away, "I know he does, sweetie. You know that I don't always agree with the things he does or the way he thinks. Sometimes I even get really pissed at him, but I know in my heart that your dad cares, and that he's trying to do what he thinks is right."

Cindy smiles; I know it's because Mom said "pissed," and Mom never talks like that.

Paul is still mad. "Sure he cares," Paul says sarcastically, "about himself!"

As I sit here listening, I realize that I agree with both Mom and Paul: I know Dad wants to help people, but I know that sometimes he's totally selfish, too. If I could talk, however, I'd say one other thing to them. I'd remind them that Dad is really sharp when it comes to money and the writing business. I know it's vulgar and crude and crass to mention filthy lucre, but Dad *does* pay for our house, our food—in fact, all of our expenses! Mom works part-time, but actually *I'm* her full-time job. Taking care of me is expensive, and Dad pays for it all. He has to think about money. With Dad's fame from the Pulitzer and the controversial subject matter of Earl Detraux, Dad probably sees a gold mine. And he's probably right.

I'm sure Detraux is a hero to a lot of people. His son had a terrible seizure condition and was retarded. Earl isn't an educated man like my dad; he worked at a gas station during the day and a pizza place at night. When he was charged with killing his son, he pled guilty. Talking from the steps of the courthouse as he was being led away, he said, "I did it. I killed him. How can I say 'not guilty'? I loved my son too much to watch him suffer anymore." Then he added that he'd killed his two-year-old son to "end my baby's pain."

I'm pretty good at adding two plus two and coming up with four. Dad's getting deeper and deeper into this whole "ending pain" stuff, which means that I'm in deeper and deeper trouble.

CHAPTER ELEVEN

Lindy and Shawn and I are alone,
her mother, gone,
our friends, gone,
and I look at Lindy
and she looks at me
and there is nothing left
for either of us to see.

On Wednesday Dad and Cindy flew to Los Angeles to tape *The Alice Ponds Show*. Paul, of course, refused to go. They flew back home on Thursday. The show is being broadcast this afternoon, Monday, at three P.M.

The Alice Ponds Show is one of the most popular programs in America. Alice appeals to an uneducated, loud audience. Actually, most times I've ever seen it, it's seemed pretty ridiculous.

Mom, Cindy, and Paul are all in the family room when it's time for the program to start. To the degree my eyes will cooperate, I'll be able to see it too, from my spot by the window.

Alice opens her show in her typical style, introducing the day's program in as controversial and outrageous a manner as she can:

"Parents who kill," she begins, shaking her head sadly. "Parents who kill. Why?"

Her audience instantly boos. What a courageous group, I sarcastically decide, they're against parents who kill their kids.

Alice presses on: "Today, Pulitzer Prize–winning poet and author Sydney E. McDaniel will be joining us, along with his daughter, Cynthia McDaniel, to discuss Mr. McDaniel's newest work in progress, his book about Earl Detraux, a man who murdered his own child."

The audience boos again at the mention of Detraux's name.

Alice, smiling inappropriately, says, "Parents who can't love their own children? Mothers and fathers who slaughter defenseless, innocent infants? The Susan Smiths, the Diane Downses, the Earl Detrauxs of the world. What can these people show us about the nature of pure evil? In today's hour we'll look at one such monster and see if we can find some answers."

I immediately remember the old news stories and TV movies: Susan Smith is that mother who backed her car into a lake in South Carolina, killing her kids and trying to blame it on "black abductors"; Diane Downs was the woman from Oregon in that old movie *Small Sacrifices* who shot her three children; and, of course, Earl Detraux, homegrown here in Washington state, from the small community of Otis Orchards, near Spokane. Earl smothered his two-year-old retarded son.

As Alice Ponds carries on, Paul hops up and walks across to the kitchen. He grabs a bag of Ruffles Mesquite Barbecue Potato Chips. Noticing that Mom's attention is glued to the TV screen, Paul pops a tiny piece of chip into my mouth as he walks past. As he does this, he looks at me and smiles, then gives me a little wink. Mom hates for him to feed me anything without my bib on, because it's a saliva free-flow disaster, but when he sees a chance to do it, Paul often sneaks me treats anyway. I truly love him for it.

Unfortunately, just as Dad and Cindy come onto the screen, I begin to feel a seizure start. It's not a real big one, more like a brain sneeze that can't quite decide whether it's going to happen or not. Still it's frustrating. Somehow I manage to keep the bite of potato chip in my mouth. This seizure is not big, but it's big enough for me not to be able to quite make out what Alice Ponds is saying on TV or how Cindy and Paul and Mom are reacting. I'm able to keep my spirit in my body, but for the first ten minutes of the program my mouth is blessed by Frito-Lay while my brain is a short-circuiting wad of useless electrical static.

When my seizure finally passes and I'm able to focus again, I realize that Alice has asked Dad a question. In fact she's still in the middle of that question when Dad cuts her off.

"You're right, Alice," Dad interrupts in a soft but firm voice. "I do love my son Shawn. I love all three of my children. I think it's impossible for others to judge whether one person loves another or not. We only know in our own hearts what we feel. Whether people believe I love my son makes little difference to me. I love Shawn. I know that Earl Detraux loved his child, Colin, too."

For an instant, the audience seems stunned. They don't know whether to applaud or throw hand grenades. As the camera scans their faces, many of them look at Alice for some kind of hint which way they should go. At first Alice is not much help; she looks as surprised as they do.

Quickly, though, Alice recovers, a serious and heavy shortness to her tone. "You think that Earl

Detraux, who murdered little Colin Detraux, *loved* his child? You honestly believe that a parent can kill a baby in the name of love?"

Now the audience knows what to do. They hoot, they howl, they bark like dogs.

But before Alice can argue any more with him, Dad begins to speak again. "Everybody wants to love their kids," he says, his voice soft, reassuring. "Nobody sets out to be a bad parent." Alice's audience begins to quiet down; they're like dumb beasts, hypnotized by the gentle sound of Dad's voice. "Yet thousands of children are hurt every year by their parents, parents who behave as though they *hate* their kids."

The camera pans the audience. Literally dozens of people, tiny heads on tiny bodies, nod in agreement.

Dad has them. "I really believe that everybody in this room loves their children, and that everybody who is not yet a parent but will be someday will love their children too. But has anyone here ever spent months or years of your lives watching your child suffer the most horrifying, excruciating torture imaginable? Have you ever wondered if a definition of love might not include taking responsibility for someone who cannot take responsibility for his or her self?"

The audience is now dead quiet, staring at Dad and listening. Dad takes a long, slow breath, the first one he's had since he started talking. He looks out into the audience as if quietly daring anyone to contradict him.

Dad goes on. "We all know, all of us who are parents, that sometimes we hurt our children out of love. We know that telling a child 'no' when that child is desperate to hear 'yes' causes sadness. But when that 'yes' could cause them harm or endanger them, a good parent takes responsibility by saying 'no,' regardless of how upset our child might feel—"

Alice attempts to interrupt. "I think—"

Dad ignores her: "The point is that we *do* have to make hard choices every day to be good parents, to truly take responsibility for our children. If we love them enough, we say 'no,' we let them feel their hurt or sadness or rage, but we stand firm and do what has to be done."

The audience begins to applaud in spite of itself. It's as if they can't stop themselves from applauding, from agreeing with something that they don't quite understand, but that makes too much sense to ignore.

Alice turns to a woman in the audience to let her ask a question. The woman is short and fat and kind of crazy-looking. "Don't you think that Detraux is just a stupid killer? Don't you think that he deserved to be the one to die?"

Dad stares at the woman and without hesitation

responds, "Have you ever said to anybody something like 'If I'm ever brain damaged and in a coma, just put me out of my misery?'"

"What?" the woman asks, blinking nervously.

Dad presses on, "I mean, I think most people have said things like that. I know I have, and I know friends have said things like that to me. If you were unable to kill yourself but you wanted to be dead, don't you think you'd want somebody to know your wishes?"

Alice, pretending to be real concerned but actually sounding phony to me, says, "I'm not sure that's really the point, Syd. We're not here today to discuss voluntary euthanasia."

Dad sighs and shakes his head. "You're right, Alice. Let's keep that focus nice and tight. To answer your friend's question—what do I think about Detraux? I think he was a man who did what he thought he had to do."

Alice looks at Dad and says, "I know you've brought some video footage of interviews you've been conducting with the child killer—"

"Child killer?" Dad interrupts.

Alice burrows in. "Mr. Detraux did kill his son, didn't he?" she asks. "He was convicted of murder for that crime, wasn't he? His little boy *was* a two-year-old, utterly incapable of defending himself in any way, wasn't he?" Alice sounds confident.

Suddenly a photograph of a cute little boy, a blowup of a snapshot, grainy, a kind of orange tint over the color, fills the screen.

Alice says, "We're showing our audience a snapshot of little Colin right now."

The audience *oohs* and *ahhs* for a moment, then snaps to silence as they realize this was Earl Detraux's victim.

Alice, certain that nothing can go wrong, asks, "Earl did kill this little angel, didn't he?"

Dad looks at her and quietly says, "No, he didn't."

Alice looks genuinely confused, almost stunned. "That *is* Colin Detraux, isn't it?"

Dad answers, "Yes, that *was* him."

"*Was*, because his father murdered him."

"No," Dad answers. "Colin died from a terrible, terminal, inoperable seizure disorder, an irreversible medical condition, coupled with profound mental retardation that made his existence insufferable."

"His father—" Alice begins, but Dad cuts her off.

"His father loved him enough to do whatever he had to do to end his son's suffering. Earl loved his son enough to sacrifice his own life to end his child's pain—"

"Including murder," Alice interrupts.

"Why don't we let Earl speak for himself?" Dad asks softly.

"Indeed," Alice says. "Are we ready to roll the

tape?" A couple seconds later, Alice says, "We are? Good. Roll please."

On the screen appears an image of Earl Detraux. I have seen him before, but I am curious about his appearance now, since he's been in prison. Luckily my eyes are focused on him. He is sitting in front of a gray wall, in an orange-colored inmate's jumpsuit. I can't tell how tall he is, but he looks about the same size as Dad. His face is pleasant. His hair is cut quite short and he's mostly bald on top. His left ear sticks out a little farther than the right. Otherwise he's regular-looking with a mild, gap-toothed smile. He sure doesn't look like any murderer I've ever seen in movies or on TV crime shows. Just the opposite— he looks like a next-door neighbor, a guy you'd see out mowing his lawn or raking his leaves, Mr. Average.

The way the prison room is set up, Dad is sitting next to Earl; their metal folding chairs almost touch, but both men face more toward the camera than toward one another. They are framed on-screen from the ankles up. They look comfortable, if not quite relaxed.

DAD: Tell us about life here, Earl.

EARL: Well, it's probably not like you'd expect it to be. Most guys keep pretty much to themselves. If you want to know about bad stuff, you can find out about it; if you want to stay out of people's way and just mind your own business, you can do that.

That's been my approach so far. It's sort of like Scout camp, only there's a lot more tattoos.

DAD: *(Smiles, then pauses and grows serious.)* We came to talk about your son, Earl, about Colin and what happened to him. Are you ready to discuss that?

EARL: *(Swallows hard and stares down at his hands, crossed in his lap.)* It's hard, but yeah, I'm ready.

DAD: Why did you kill him, Earl?

EARL: Nobody will ever understand this. I'm not saying it to be understood. I'm saying it because it's true and because you have a son like Colin. Maybe it'll help you and other people with children like Colin. I don't feel now and I will never feel that I killed or murdered Colin. I did what I did with my son to end his suffering. *(Earl pauses a moment and takes several slow, deep breaths. He looks up at Dad. The camera slowly closes in on his face.)*

If you love your child enough and you see him suffering horribly, and you know, both medically, 'cause of what the docs tell you, and in your heart, that his condition is hopeless, and that his life is nothing but pain and agony—if you love him enough, what do you do? Colin was helpless. It was like he was in the hands of invisible demons whose only reason for existing was to torture him. *(A tear slowly slips out of the corner of Earl Detraux's left eye.*

He wipes it off his cheek with the back of his right hand.)

It had to stop. I didn't care about what the laws or the cops or anybody else had to say about it . . . hell, they didn't know, they weren't there watching Colin, they weren't in his head or in my heart. I didn't care about what could happen to me. It had to stop. I loved Colin. I still love him and I'll always love him. Ending his suffering was all I cared about. I did that, and whatever anybody else thinks of me, I feel that what I did is between me and Colin and his mother and our God.

DAD: If you had it to do over again, would you do it?

EARL: *(Smiles a little.)* I guess I'm supposed to say, "No sir, I've learned my lesson." I mean, I would like to get out this place someday, so I'm supposed to say that I know what I did was wrong . . . but the truth is I'd do it again this second. I'd do it every day they let me out if I saw Colin suffering. Yeah, I'd do it again.

DAD: What if next week they invented a new medication or a new procedure that could have cured Colin? How would you live with yourself if that happened?

EARL: Well, the docs said that wasn't going to happen, but if it did, how would I feel? How will I feel if, at the end of my life, I'm cast down into Hell for all eternity for what I did?

(Earl smiles sadly and looks away from the camera. He pauses and takes a sip from a glass of water on a table off camera, then sets the glass back down. He takes a deep breath.)

You know, when I did it, I put the pillow over Colin's face and held it there, not hard so as to hurt him, but just enough to cut off the air. I held the pillow and I prayed as hard as I could. I hoped God might intervene, like he did with Abraham, when he provided a ram and spared Isaac. Only I wasn't praying for God to stop me; I was praying that Colin wasn't suffering. He didn't struggle against me at all. He was real still and quiet the whole time. *(Earl pauses again and breathes slowly, steadying himself.)*

I prayed for God to let Colin's suffering end and to take care of him for me. When it was over, when I felt Colin go, he lay there like an angel, so beautiful, and I could tell that for the first time in his life, I knew in my heart, that for the first time in his life he was without pain. I looked into his eyes and saw that he was gone. For the first time ever, I saw peace in his face. *(Earl looks up and tears stream down both his cheeks. He is finished talking. His face, although tear streaked, looks calm and peaceful. He sits straight, with dignity and quiet pride.)*

DAD: Thank you for talking to us, Earl. That's enough for today. *(The camera clicks off and the screen goes blank.)*

We are suddenly back to Alice Ponds, who stands quietly for a moment, then speaks, her voice full of emotion. "We'll be right back."

Our family room is utterly silent. I can hear Mom breathing. I see Paul and Cindy, speechless, staring vacantly at the TV as a lady on the screen talks about the bright whiteness of her wash. No one looks at me.

I think about Earl and Colin, about Dad and me. What good is love if it isn't about putting somebody else ahead of yourself? I don't think Earl was playing God when he killed Colin. He believed that loving his son meant ending the kid's suffering by any means necessary. Earl's action and Dad's decision to study it convince me more than ever that Dad is still working out what he should do with me. Dad knows that Earl loved his son, just like Dad loves me. I have this feeling, a gut feeling, so real that I can't deny it, that right now Dad is trying to find a reason, any reason, *not* to kill me.

But before Alice Ponds and her astonished audience and my dad and my sister and another commercial and all the rest can come back, the seizure

I fought off a little while ago charges back into my head. There's no stopping it this time as it begins its march up my spine, down my arms, and across my forehead. *Crackle—crackle—crackle*—that's all the Alice Ponds I'm going to get today.

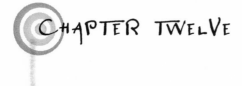

CHAPTER TWELVE

Months break over us.
Shawn is dead,
only he eats, breathes, defecates,
trapped inside some kind of being
that no one will ever
understand.

This seizure is a doozy. I hear Alice Ponds mumbling some questions to Cindy on the TV, but I find it impossible to stick around. Soon I am floating over the roof of our house, soaring up and down, eyeing the landscape, not really feeling anything—you can't feel without your body—but *experiencing* everything in me and around me as pure joy.

I love my mom, brother, sister, dad. Although I can't connect with things through my senses, there is an energy inside me and around me; somehow all the things I think about and remember turn to joy. Pure joy: favorite movies, paintings I've seen and loved, music on compact discs, pinecones, chocolate pudding, the taste of smoked oysters (thank you, Paul!), the sound of motors, a bright-red 1966 Ford Mustang. I love the idea of books and the dusty smell of them on bookshelves, the scent of Comet in a stainless steel sink. I think of the way, on cool mornings in November, the sun pours in through the window, and covers my hands. I think about my baths every night with Mom dripping warm water from a big soft sponge down my back, the hairbrush passing through my hair after the tangles are all gone, all of it turning to joy. Life can be great, even for me. Even for me.

I begin a slow, easy weave around the sky above our house and Mom's little garden. I soar, glide. I know with a certainty beyond all doubt that I am a part of all of this and that I belong here. I don't want to die! I want to live! I want to stay here and . . .

I wake up in my body, tired. I never remember the actual moment of my shift back into myself from a seizure. One second my spirit is out surfing cumulus clouds or playing with the wind, and the next moment I'm back in my body again, awake, exhausted, "real."

This time as I arrive back in my body, I realize that I'm still in my wheelchair, in my usual spot, but the TV's been turned off. Mom has left the room. Cindy and Paul are talking quietly, seriously. The first few words they speak, I can't understand them. It sounds like they are talking with mouths full of sawdust. It's not them, of course; it's just that sometimes it takes a few moments for my senses to come back online after I've been outside myself.

Finally, I understand Paul saying, "He doesn't have the guts. He wouldn't do it."

Cindy answers, "I know he wouldn't; I don't think it's about courage, though."

"No," Paul says, "maybe not. But Detraux was willing to give up his whole life for it. Dad's too selfish for that. Besides, if Dad were willing to do that, why would he have waited so long?"

Cindy pauses a moment. "Maybe he needed somebody like Detraux to show him the possibility?"

Paul thinks a moment about it. "Maybe," he says. He pauses, then speaks again, slowly; he seems to be picking his words carefully. "I liked what you said to Alice Ponds about Shawn, about how hard it is."

I realize that Paul is talking about a part of *The Alice Ponds Show* that I missed while in my seizure.

Cindy says, "I always feel so guilty complaining about it at all!"

Paul nods agreement. "Yeah, I know."

They are both quiet for a moment.

I've never heard them talk about me like this before. It doesn't really hurt my feelings. I mean, I've always thought that they must feel bad about me sometimes. Still, it surprises me. I wonder how many other times they've had talks like this one.

"Anyway," Paul says, "you were great on the show. The things you said about how Shawn's condition affected us all, how it changed us forever, that was such a great way to put it."

Cindy smiles, then speaks in a real stupid, nasal type tone, "Do you wanna kill your bruvver, too?" I can tell that Cindy is imitating one of Alice's audience members.

Paul bursts out laughing. "Wasn't she amazing? You wonder if she spells it b-r-u-v-v-e-r." He pauses, then laughs again. "And you asked, 'Which brother?' That was classic."

Cindy laughs too. "You should have seen Alice Ponds' face then, I mean off camera. I thought she'd faint."

They are quiet for a few moments. Finally Cindy speaks softly, as though wanting to be sure that Mom can't hear. "So you think Dad's all right? You think Shawn's safe?"

My ears perk up at that one. They are talking about my safety. They're thinking the same things I've been thinking.

"Yeah, Shawn's safe," Paul says, sure and definite. "Even if Dad's gone nuts and wants to do something, he'd have to come through me."

Cindy nods. She knows what that means. Actually, we both do.

One day last summer I was out on our front porch sitting in my wheelchair. Paul, grounded that day, had missed the chance to meet friends at the Queen Anne cinema to take in a matinee. He'd stayed out too late the night before, and his punishment had been house arrest and rock-garden weeding. He was not in a very good mood. The rock garden starts at the front of our house and goes around the side. It's flat in front and sloping on the side, filled with small plants: pansies, hens-and-chickens, I don't know all the names. It looks hard to weed, uncomfortable and awkward. Never having weeded myself, I can't say for sure, but the amount of time Paul spends grunting, groaning, swearing, and stopping to stretch his back always makes the job look miserable.

Paul worked around the side of the house when two guys, both about his age, fifteen or so at that time, walked up the sidewalk to wait for the bus just outside our fence. My head/neck/eyes were not co-operating at all that afternoon, so I managed only a slight glimpse of the two strangers when they got to the bus stop. They joked together for a few moments, swearing a lot, loud and cocky. One of them said some mean-sounding stuff about a girl; the other one laughed.

"Hey," I heard one of them yell in my direction. "You know if the bus has come by or not?"

His voice sounded nervous, even a little short, as though he felt angry with me.

When I didn't answer, the same voice snapped, "Hey! You there, Roller Derby." He must have meant my wheelchair. "Has the bus come by or not?"

His friend laughed and said, "I think he's the short, stupid type."

"No duh," snarled the one who'd spoken first.

In the brief glance I'd had of them, one looked big and heavy. He wore a black T-shirt, black jeans, and boots. His friend was shorter but muscular and tough, his T-shirt a mesh muscle-type shirt that showed off his body. He stood about Paul's height, three or four inches shorter than his big friend; they both looked rough: dirty hands, scruffy long hair, a little scary.

"Hey, Ricky Retardo? Where's the bus?" said the other voice.

"Yeah," the first voice laughed, "Retardo Montobon, where's that streetcar named desire?"

They both laughed. I'd have laughed too if I could. I thought their references were pretty witty. But then the first one said, "Why don't we come up there and slap you around till you show a little respect?" He sounded mad, mean.

"Yeah," said the other voice. "If you can give us one good reason why we shouldn't mess you up a little, we'll leave your ugly ass alone. Otherwise . . ." He didn't finish his sentence.

His friend laughed again. None of their laughter sounded happy. Although I couldn't see them, I heard them come in through the gate. My spot on the porch was only ten paces from the sidewalk. They were standing right in front of me before I knew it.

"Hello, Ricky," the first of the voices said. "Seen any buses around here? What on earth are you?" he asked, flipping his finger against my nose. "He looks like some kind of cartoon geek. You're one messed-up geek there, bud."

A moment later I felt a warm sensation under my chin. It turned from warm to hot very quickly. My brain stem started twitching me around. I heard them both laugh.

"Don't like the hot stuff, hey, Mr. Wizard? Can you say 'Bic lighter' . . . ?"

That was the last word that voice said.

I managed to catch only a glimpse of Paul as he came at them from around the corner. He moved so fast that he was just a blur. Their bodies seemed to explode when he hit them. I heard a muffled cry from one of the strangers and a huge gasp from the other. For the next minute the world filled with the sound of fists hammering into flesh. Within a matter of seconds I heard only the whimpering of one of the strangers, complete silence from the other.

My head and eyes shifted, focusing over and beyond them, but even my out-of-focus view saw something horrible. The bigger guy did not move at all, just lay facedown in a puddle of blood. It looked like he'd been shot in the face, not Hollywood or TV "shot in the face," but really shot. I thought he might be dead. The smaller guy looked even bloodier than his friend did; his left nostril looked torn open. One of his eyebrows looked half torn off too, and his nose looked flattened, his eyes bloodshot. He was terrified.

The worst sight of all was Paul. He looked like a machine, pounding away at the guy still standing, turning away from him only long enough to kick and stomp the unconscious guy who lay motionless on the ground. I'd never seen such an expression on Paul's face before: The veins in his neck looked ready to pop; his fists, already dirty from the weeding, were covered with blood. He looked like a monster, barely recognizable.

In another few moments the shorter guy fell to the ground too, curling into a ball, whimpering next to his unconscious friend.

Paul ran to the side of the house, leaving them there at my feet. I could hear the smaller one muttering, "Adam, wake up . . . Adam, please . . . oh God."

In only a few seconds, Paul came back.

"You like fire, huh?" he muttered, so low and cold that it scared even me. "You're going to walk up to my brother and burn him? You think you're going to do that?" He kicked each of them, hard.

"Burn my brother?"

It wasn't until then that I saw the gasoline can Paul had brought back with him. He lifted it up, quickly unscrewed the lid, and poured the contents onto them. The fumes almost knocked me out; waves of gas shimmered up from their backs.

"You're going to burn my brother and laugh?" Paul said as he finished emptying the can. He reached down and grabbed the arm of the smaller stranger. The guy began to whimper and tried to hide his hand under himself, but Paul jerked his arm out, then bent his fingers back until I heard a sickening crack. The Bic lighter fell to the ground. Paul picked it up.

"You like fire, huh?" Paul asked.

The guy who could still talk pleaded, "Please don't . . . please . . . oh God . . . please."

Paul grabbed the back of the guy's mesh shirt

and wadded it up, jerking it close to his other hand. The guy's body looked like a rag doll. The whole world smelled of gasoline.

Paul held the lighter against the gas-soaked wad of garment. He flicked the Bic. It didn't spark. His thumb went back to the little lever to press it once again.

I heard a scream come from behind me: "Paul!"

Cindy flew off the porch and pushed Paul, who fell back onto his butt. He was up instantly, grabbing Cindy by her shirt front. He pulled back his fist to hit her, but she screamed again, "Paul! Paul! Stop it! Stop!"

Something seemed to snap in Paul. He blinked his eyes hard and stared at Cindy for what seemed like minutes, really only a few seconds.

"Okay," Paul mumbled, his voice shaky, even a little frightened. He patted Cindy's arm. "Okay, okay."

Cindy looked down at the strangers. The big one sat up now too, both of them terrified, soaked in gas, one Bic misfire from death. They sat frozen, staring down at the ground.

Cindy said, "What's going on here?" She sounded just like Mom.

Paul's lower lip began to quiver as he spoke to Cindy. "They were going to hurt Shawn. They were going to burn him."

Cindy looked at them again and said angrily, "You better hurry up and get out of here. If I let my brother go, he'll kill you."

Without a word the two strangers managed to help each other up and scurried out our open gate. In ten seconds they were gone. We never saw them again.

I never loved and feared Paul more than in that moment.

Yes. Cindy knows what Paul means when he says that Dad would have to come through him to hurt me. Cindy understands. So do I. Yet each of us knows too that Paul can't really protect me forever. The fact is, if Dad decides that Earl Detraux is right, no one can protect me.

CHAPTER THIRTEEN

Shawn and I
are alone in the darkness.

Shawn and I are alone.

We are disappearing.
We are disappearing.

It's been five days since *The Alice Ponds Show*. Five days. I can't stop thinking about my dad. Is my father going to kill me? When? How? What's going to happen?

It's Friday afternoon. Yesterday Paul got on a bus with his teammates and drove three hundred miles to Spokane to play in a basketball tournament this weekend. He was really excited. Tomorrow morning, Saturday, Mom will go to Spokane too, driving

Cindy and a couple of her girl friends over to watch the mighty Spartans take on the Fighting Knights of Spokane's Thompson High School. I'm having trouble getting caught up in the rah-rah spirit. Dad's *Alice Ponds* appearance has me pretty freaked out. Negativity. I've almost always been able to avoid it. Right now I'm floating in an ocean of it.

I try not to think about dying, but it keeps coming back into my mind. I bet condemned guys on death row feel like this, terrible, hopeless. My stomach is empty, my chest struggles to catch a breath, my thoughts are racing. I don't want to feel sorry for myself. Negativity and self-pity are useless. Mostly, all my life, I've relied on humor and remembering good stuff to get me through each day. To me laughter and memory have always been the best things to fight off worry. And after all, when you're talking memories, I *am* the king.

Right now I can't shut my memories down. My life races through my brain, and I remember everything. I can't even slow my brain down. I remember Christmas morning when I was six years old. I woke up to the sounds of Paul and Cindy in the living room. It might have been the last Christmas all three of us were still pretty much little kids. Lying in my crib, I could hear Cindy and Paul laughing. I'd hear the slightest *ripppp* and the rustling of wrapping paper, then *ooh* and *ahhh* in loud, excited whispers.

Then I'd hear them tear a piece of Scotch tape from the little plastic dispenser. They were sneaking peeks at all their gifts, then taping the presents shut again. December that year was fairly warm. I remember lying there in my crib and a robin, very fat, came and landed on the sill outside my window. I saw him through a small crack between the curtains. He was parked right in the middle of the opening, staring in at me. He seemed to know what was going on, like he was a member of the Christmas morning bird police. He seemed to be asking me whether or not we should bust Cindy and Paul. I knew it couldn't be true, but it felt true. I thought to the robin, Let's just let 'em go this time, and the robin winked at me, then flew away. I remember!

I remember when I was eight, Dad and Mom took the three of us kids to the Seattle Center, to the Pacific Science Center. Cindy and Paul had been begging to go to the virtual reality attraction. If you waited in line for forty minutes, you could put on headgear, step into this twirly machine, and fly through the cosmos. After Cindy and Paul had each had their turns, I figured we'd leave, but Dad said, "Shawn's turn."

The guy running the ride looked at me in my wheelchair and said, "I'm sorry, sir, I don't know how we'd put a wheelchair in this."

Dad gave the guy one of his best Sydney E.

McDaniel, Madman Poet, stares; this was in the pre-Pulitzer era, and Dad looked a lot more "mad" back then. Dad said, "I wasn't interested in taking the wheelchair for a ride." He lifted me out like I weighed one ounce, and demanded, "Strap me in. I'll hold him."

The guy running the show was tall and thin, wearing a green Science Center polo shirt. "I don't know."

"Come on, buddy," my dad said, like the guy'd been his best friend for twenty years. "You know the drill: no guts, no glory. This kid and I are one turn, look." Dad walked over to the machine, and before the guy could say another word, Dad, talking non-stop, stepped into the harness, holding me all the while, never giving the attendant a chance to say "no" again.

"This'll be great," Dad said. "Nobody wants a lawsuit over failure to serve the handicapped; everybody is happy; everybody wants to have fun. This is great. We're havin' some fun now. Great, great. Now I'll just strap in, and we'll put that headgear jobby right on old Shawn's noggin here, and we're all set."

By the time the guy could get a word out, Dad and I were already strapped into the contraption. Dad reached out, grabbed the headgear from the guy, and put it on me.

In the next moment I whirled through time and

space, stars shot past me, and the galaxy unfolded: light, darkness, speed. Fantastic! The best part of all, though: I loved the feeling of my dad's arms around me, holding me tightly as we spun and twisted our way through the universe. I remember.

I remember all my reactions to all the music I've ever heard: songs, melodies, and symphonies. I remember images too: van Gogh's *Crows in a Corn Field*, Hopper's *Nighthawks*, Picasso's *Guernica*, and Mary Randlett's photographs of water caressing stones. I remember the faces, voices, hands, and hearts of artists and poets, actors and ditch diggers, cops and grocers, the guy who reads our electric meter.

I remember Ken Burns's *Baseball*, Mom's Charlie perfume, Cindy's laughter and her smile, the blood that time on Paul's hands, and all the times I heard his laugh and the thump of his feet as he ran up the stairs, the ring of the telephone, the snap of a drum, the morning paper hitting the porch. I remember: Ally's pretty face, William's strong arms, Becky's soft smile, "winky, winky, winky." My life moves across the back of my eyes, across the middle of my ears, and everything I've ever dreamed, seen, smelled, heard, desired, loved, hated, been scared of, wished I could touch—I remember all of it.

Memory is all we have, for ourselves and for the

people we love. The memories of us, once we die, are all that's left of us. When I'm gone, maybe someone will pick up my dad's poem "Shawn"; maybe it will be a year after I'm dead, maybe two years, maybe two hundred years. Maybe that person will read the poem and be moved and think they know me. Whom will they know? What will they know? Will that edition carry a special note explaining that Sydney E. McDaniel, the author of the poem, killed his son? Will the reader know Dad or me any better? If I'm anything at all, you'd have to agree that I am memory. Will anyone ever know that my life, once lived and then over, was one of perfect remembering? No one will know. No one will know me. I'm just not ready to give up the hope that someday I might be known. I'm not ready.

CHAPTER FOURTEEN

In sleep, voice quiet, he breathes,
hands still, in silence, slumbering.
His spirit is a feather on a quiet river. . . .

It's about ten o'clock at night. I'm tired. Remembering all your lifetime of memories and thinking about being dead all day long is hard work. I fall asleep right away. I begin to dream.

In my dream I'm at my dad's place, his little green house surrounded and overgrown by trees that hide it from the street. It's just a simple little two-story home, two bedrooms, one bathroom. It has a deck in front, built around a huge old cherry tree.

Suddenly I'm in Dad's bedroom, next to him as he sleeps. I've visited this room many times during my seizure travels: I can see, on the wall, through the darkness, framed photographs of me, Cindy, Paul, the three of us together and apart; there's one picture taken when all three of us were just little kids and Dad had hair and Mom looked like a kid herself.

In one corner of the room, just below a tall window that looks out toward the street, is a writing table; Dad's computer sits on it. His screensaver pattern is dots of light rushing toward us—they look like stars falling off the sides and top and bottom before they fly off the screen. I slip back into the darkest corner of the room, next to the closet door, and wedge myself into the blackness.

Finally I gather my courage, approach Dad's bed, and whisper gently, "Dad." He doesn't respond.

"Hey, come here," I command, so sharply that I even scare myself. In that instant Dad looks up at me.

He stares into my eyes, confusion playing across his face—he seems to be trying to place me.

"I don't know you," he says. "Are you an angel?"

"No," I answer, a little shocked that we are actually talking.

"Dad, it's me," I say, realizing that these are the first words he's ever heard me speak.

"Oh my baby," Dad whispers, and begins to weep. "Oh baby boy, you're gone. Oh God, I'm so sorry you're gone."

"Dad, it's okay. I'm okay."

"Oh God, Shawn, you're gone."

I interrupt, speaking firmly, "Dad, I'm right here, I love you, I need you to know—"

Ignoring me, Dad interrupts. "I'm so sorry I lost you, baby, I'm so sorry I had to let you go. You were my baby, my baby boy, and I said good-bye, I left you and I lost you." Dad sobs.

"Dad, it's all right," I insist, trying to interrupt; I want to comfort him.

Dad says, "You're gone, you became an angel because I let you go. Double-jointed thumbs, just you and me. I had to let go. . . ." His tears choke off the rest of his words.

I begin to cry too. "Dad, Daddy . . . I . . . I can't." I'm crying too hard to speak.

"I'm so sorry, baby boy," Dad says, his voice trembling, slicing into me like a scalpel carving an aching loss.

"You're an angel, baby boy. The angels came and loved you away because I let you go.

"Good-bye, son," he says softly. "Good-bye, baby boy. Go be an angel."

"I love you, Dad," I say, and in the instant before the dream ends, I add desperately, "I don't want to die!"

CHAPTER FIFTEEN

Inside me this moment changes
into something never felt before;
a flutter of feathers as two birds, falling,
pass down through a blind, silent prayer,
whispering good-bye to dreams and hope,
pass down, falling, and whispering good-bye.

It's Saturday morning. Surrounded by sleeping bags,
coolers, suitcases, cosmetics kits, groceries, noise,
laughter, and the high-pitched chatter of female
voices, Cindy, her friends, and Mom are doing the
last-minute preparations for their trip to Spokane.
Go, Spartans!

After what seems like hours the van is finally
packed. Mom stops to give me a kiss on the forehead

as she moves toward the door. But before her lips can even pucker up, Cindy, laughing, pulls her away. And suddenly they're gone. In a burst of energy and collective chaos, they're out the door.

Vonda, my respite care provider, is nice. As near as I can tell, "respite care provider" is a fancy name for baby-sitter. She's taken care of me before. She's a little impatient at my feeding times, and I'm sure when she has to change my diapers, she comes up with lots of better ideas for making six bucks an hour. But most of the day she watches TV, chats on the phone, and reads *Good Housekeeping* or *Glamour*, which she has brought along with her. She doesn't give me much attention, but then nobody else does either.

Today she's happy. She's working on her nails, glopping on deep-purple polish, followed by a sprinkling of gold glitter. She's at least, league minimum, fifty pounds overweight, but her nails and her hair are perfect. I like her. Later tonight she'll feed me, then give me my meds. She'll put me in my pajamas, making sure I'm dry and clean; then she'll put me to bed.

The day goes by so fast. Each hour seems like a minute. Whenever I manage to focus on the digital clock on the microwave in the kitchen, I'm shocked by how much time has passed.

It's already early afternoon by the time I have my first seizure.

Outside of my body I decide to take a little tour of Seattle: Pike Place Market, the Seattle Art Museum, Pioneer Square, the waterfront with its cheesy piers and stench of fishy salt water.

I take this seizure slowly. I consider soaring down I-90 to see if I can spot Mom's van. But in my spirit I don't feel like flying or soaring or zipping across time and space. I feel relaxed, content. I float aimlessly; I am at peace. I think about all the things I remember, I think about all the things I've heard, and I wonder if . . .

I'm back in my body again. One second I was in Elliot Bay Bookstore, floating my way between the pages of some favorite old picture books, and the next I am in my bed. It's dark out already. I must have slept for hours.

I hear a car pull up. One door opens, then slams shut. I hear footsteps approaching the house. There is a knock on the front door, but then someone walks on in.

"Hello," I hear Dad call.

"Hi," Vonda calls back.

"It's Shawn's father."

"All right," Vonda answers. I hear an edge of excitement in her tone.

They exchange pleasantries in the entryway: Dad comments on her nails, she thanks him, a giggly blush to her voice.

Dad asks, "How was Shawn's day?"

"Oh, just fine," Vonda answers. "It's so exciting to meet you. I read your poem, about Shawn . . . I mean, of course, the one about Shawn . . . I mean . . . it was *so* wonderful . . . I'm *so* honored. I always hoped I'd meet you."

She sounds literally breathless, but she manages to go on. "I even have your book with me—I mean in my purse. I always bring it in the hope that I might . . . I mean that you might . . . what I mean is, would you autograph it for me?"

I can hear the smile in Dad's voice as he answers, "Sure."

I hear a brief rummaging, as Vonda digs into her purse. Then I hear Dad speak. His voice has a slightly distracted sound to it. "I was thinking," Dad says casually, "that I'd like to stay over tonight with Shawn. You've already fed him and put him to bed, right?"

"Oh yes," Vonda answers. "Will you write 'To Vonda Quarantos,' then something kind of personal?" She giggles, embarrassed.

"Of course," Dad says, then, while inscribing her book, in the same casual, off-the-cuff tone, he adds, "I was just thinking, there's no sense in your being trapped here all night. I'll stay with Shawn."

"Are you sure?" Vonda asks.

"Absolutely. You'll still get paid for the hours, of course, but I'm not doing anything else tonight, and I'm happy to help out."

"Gosh," Vonda says. "That'd be great."

Dad says, "It's a done deal."

I realize that in all my years of being alive, my dad has never before stayed with me all by himself overnight. Yet suddenly he's volunteered to take care of me.

A done deal, huh? Am I the done deal?

CHAPTER SIXTEEN

We sat in that silent darkness,
I felt my baby dreaming.
His breath was Lindy and me saying good-bye.
His breath was my grandfather's breathing,
his breath was my father loving us,
his breath was my breath, we breathed as one.

I hear Dad come into the room. I wait calmly. There's nothing else I can do. I'm not afraid. My breathing is easy. I feel steady, relaxed, and alert. Whatever my dad has decided, whatever he decides—I can't know whether it's right or wrong, because I don't really know what is for the best; maybe death is nothing like I saw that day when that dog died. Maybe death is simply flying free forever. I just don't know.

"Hey, buddy," Dad says. He comes to my bed,

lowers the side, and sits next to me. He's quiet. He reaches down to the foot of my bed in the corner where a quilted pillow lies. He grabs the pillow and sets it in his lap. My eyes happen to focus on the pillow. Mom made the quilted cover years ago, maybe even before Dad left us. There's a pattern of checkered blocks, light blue and off-white, and a thin band of dark burgundy along the edge. That dark-reddish band of color reminds me of the way blood looks in black-and-white movies. I'm remembering a part of Dad's poem, the night he almost ended it all. I remember Earl Detraux's description of killing his son.

Dad says, his eyes sad, "I hope you know I love you. I've always loved you." He pauses, careful in his words. I can tell he's rehearsed some of this. He shifts the pillow nervously in his lap, his hands kneading the cushion. He reaches over, takes my hands. "Double-jointed," he says, setting them on the pillow on his lap. He gently bends my thumbs into right angles, bends his own too. "Just you and me."

I think the words "I love you too, Dad," trying to will them into his mind.

Dad breathes slowly, staring at our hands. He's trying to maintain control, fighting back his tears and looking at me. "Shawn, I've always loved you," he repeats, his voice soft and trembling. The weight of his words and thoughts seems to tug on him like a necklace of concrete blocks. He squeezes the pillow hard, blood draining from his knuckles. "I know I say 'I love you' too easily, and that the words collapse in meaning when they're said too many times. But no one will ever know what I mean by 'love' as I say it to you, unless that person has gone through what we have, unless he's going through it right now." Dad breaks down. Through soft sobs he struggles to get the words out. I hear his words. "Never does a day go by when I don't think about you. Never does an hour pass when I don't wonder how you are, how you're feeling. The word 'love' doesn't touch what I feel about you, for you." He pauses, regaining his composure.

I will the words "I love you too" over and over.

My eyes happen to shift to his face; I watch his expression as he talks. I've never noticed before how much older he's getting. His skin is smooth and he's still handsome, but he looks almost frail. His eyes look like they've seen too much sadness; the creases around them are deep.

He says, "When I think about you, Shawn, my heart breaks at one moment and is at peace the next. When I think about you hurting, I can barely even breathe, my chest aches so badly. I sometimes pray, Just let this all be over." He seems suddenly stronger again, almost angry as he adds, "When you were born, and we were told that you'd have these kinds of problems, do you know I got down on my knees and prayed harder than I'd ever prayed, begging God or Satan, or anybody in between, to let me trade places with you? I prayed, night after night, that I could be the one trapped inside your body and that you could take my place. I prayed so hard, for weeks, months, that I almost started believing in God." He laughs at his irony. "I guess we know how that worked out." His voice turns hard. "I could never find words strong enough to express the hate I felt toward God when those prayers went unanswered. It took years for me to sign in on *that* armistice. God was patient." He sighs.

"Nothing is ever easy, is it, Shawn? Nothing is ever like it seems. You know none of us really knows you. I mean, it takes just as much faith on our part to believe that you're retarded as it would to believe that you're a genius." He chuckles a little at that one. "Well, maybe genius is pushing it, but you know what I mean? What if you understand everything? What if you know what I've been thinking of doing, but you can't do anything about it?" He searches for the right words; I see the pain in his face and body, shoulders down, neck stiff, his hands quivering. "So many answers you can't provide, but does that mean you don't understand the questions? What would you tell me to do, Shawn? I dreamed about you the other night. I dreamed that you talked to me—I can't remember what you said. Were you happy? Sad? I can't remember. . . ."

He seems tired from all his words. "I don't know what to do, son," he says, his voice exhausted. I watch his chest rise. It's as though he is lifting himself up one last time. A final stand? I see the pillow in his lap. He pauses and takes a deep, slow breath. Has it all come down to this? With his thumbnail he unconsciously tugs at a loose thread on one corner of the pillow, sliding the thread over and over between the nail and the flesh.

My eyes have been shifting all over the place, but now suddenly, as if by some miracle, I look up directly at my dad. Our eyes lock. I see in my father's expression that he is staring back at me. We are somehow together again, like that night in my dream when we spoke. Dad stares not just at me, but into me. In all my life we have never been like this before.

"Shawn?" he says softly. "Son . . ." he begins. Tears come back into his eyes again as we sit in this strange, impossible moment. "I love you," Dad says again.

I call the words out silently, from the deepest part of my heart, "I love you too, Dad," wishing I could say it, wishing he could hear!

But before either of us can speak again, I feel

crackle—crackle—crackle. I can't tell what's going to happen next. My seizure begins to spin slowly through me. What will my dad do? Whatever it is, in another moment I'll be flying free. Either way, whatever he does, I'll be soaring.

AUTHOR'S NOTE

Some writers invent a story and their characters, making us believe in the world they've imagined. Other stories are based on "real" events that a writer has lived through.

Stuck in Neutral is neither one nor the other but a blend of both types. While I invented Shawn's world and made up all the things that happen, I also based what I wrote on my being the parent of a kid like Shawn, my son Henry Sheehan Trueman.

Sheehan is perceived very much the way Shawn is seen by the people in this story—that is, as incapable of learning or understanding much of anything. Sheehan, like Shawn, has cerebral palsy, cannot communicate at all, and has been diagnosed as being profoundly developmentally disabled. He is often called retarded, a retardate, or even worse, a retard.

In writing *Stuck in Neutral*, I wanted to invent a character, and how the world might be for that character, based on what life might be like for my son Sheehan. Is Sheehan a secret genius, like Shawn in this story? Does he like potato chips and rock and roll? Inside himself is he witty and funny and wise? Is he happy to be alive?

I can't say "yes" to any of these questions. But I can't say "no" either. All anybody can honestly say is "I don't know"—none of us really does.

6/00

CB
2/02